J.S. TORRES

The Bloodstone

The Leaf and the Tree of Old

First published by Muddlog 2020

First edition

ISBN: 978-0-578-70123-3

Cover art by Gerardo Betancourt

This book was professionally typeset on Reedsy. Find out more at reedsy.com

For my family who never gave up on me, and for the friends who became family. Thank you for all of your love, support and inspiration. Without you, I would not be here. I would also like to dedicate this story to anyone who has suffered from an anxiety disorder and agoraphobia. Stay Strong.

"Courage is not the absence of fear, it is the ability to act in the presence of fear."

- Bruce Lee

I

Part One

1

Nothingness

"Death comes to us all." Those were words his Grandmother had once told him, and a phrase that had haunted him since he was a child. Growing up, Laik spent most of his time either playing outside or trying to earn his older brother's acceptance. Vidion, who was nearly ten years older than Laik, was an angry and overly jealous young man. He hated Laik for having come into the world at all, and especially for the fact that his father was also now a part of the family, whereas Vidion's was not. The fact that he had been the result of his mother's rape, by a traveler, did not matter to Vidion. In his mind, his mother, Myla, should have stayed alone, but no one in this world wants to be alone. It is human nature to need and seek affection.

Years after she was raped, a young man by the name of Quinn captured her attention and healed her broken heart. He was a kind, gentle, and thoughtful man and most, if not all, of the villagers respected him. Quinn took it upon himself to help raise Vidion, even though Vidion resented him. As soon as he was old enough, Quinn began to teach him how to wield a sword, hunt, and take care of himself and his family. Vidion learned everything a person needed to survive through Quinn, yet never once managed to say the words "Thank you." He spent most of his time giving him a hard time in hopes that he would leave Myla and never return, but Quinn never budged. He loved Myla, and he loved Vidion, despite his faults.

After years of trying, Myla found herself expecting a sibling for Vidion. It was her dream to provide Vidion with a brother or sister to play with, and she felt that it would be good for him. Unbeknownst to her, the idea only further infuriated him. To him, it meant less attention. It suggested, he thought, that his mother would not love him as much. It also meant that Quinn would now be in the picture forever; but out of those three thoughts, the only one that proved to be true was that Quinn would never betray Myla, and he would never leave them. Before long, Myla gave birth to Laik, an event which Vidion had hoped would never come. Even though he did not believe in the gods, Vidion prayed every night and wished for a miscarriage; but his prayer was not answered. As he grew, Laik began to look up to his older brother. He was, however, not a positive influence for him, and things only got worse as Laik got older. Once Laik was old enough to walk, speak, understand, and communicate, Vidion began to carefully manipulate and bully his little brother. He was careful not to get caught by Quinn or his mother, and cautious not to allow Laik to suspect his ill intentions.

"If you want to be around me, you have to be quicker. I've seen Grandma Elona move faster than this, and if you don't hurry, we won't make it back with enough time for her to tell you one of her stupid fake stories," Vidion grumbled as he trotted further from Laik.

They were on their way back from collecting firewood for

the night, which would normally have taken them a fraction of the time they had taken today. Vidion had played the fool and taken a longer route to ensure he did not have to hear one of his grandmother's bedtime stories. Additionally, Vidion had convinced Laik that his shoulder was hurting and he would not be able to carry the firewood. Of course, Laik saw this as an opportunity to help his family, and volunteered to carry the wood himself. It was times like this that he longed to show his older brother that he was not as useless as he always told him. It was also the only way he thought he would make it on time for Elona's bedtime stories. Her stories were usually filled with mystical adventure, something Vidion hated and Laik loved. It was Laik's favorite part of the day. The rest of the villagers at Toewood thought of Elona as a crazy old lady with nothing better to do than spread false stories and false cheer. Still, they also knew that she was harmless and cared for them all. Right before bedtime, Elona would gather all of the children of Toewood and share a story about the days the gods had roamed their lands. It was either that, or about a monster that had once lurked in their forests. It was stories like these that made Laik want to grow up to be as brave, respected, and strong as his father.

As the boys approached Toewood, Vidion began to stretch his shoulder and move it around. "What a miracle!" Vidion exclaimed. "My shoulder. It feels fine. Let me take the wood the rest of the way. I should be fine, and you could use a break. You did a fine job, Laik." Laik was relieved. Although he was much smaller and younger than his brother, he'd managed to carry the heavy load of firewood over four miles of all sorts of terrain. His body was weary and shaking. Vidion tried to hide the smirk that formed on his face as he watched his brother struggle. By the time they got to the house, Vidion had grabbed the wood, and carried it in as if he were the one who put in the hard labor. "Mother. I'm exhausted. It was a rough search for the wood, and the way back was perilous," Vidion explained. Meanwhile, Laik was looking desperately through the front window, searching for someone. Quinn smiled and asked, "What is so important this late at night that must be found at this moment? Is it one of your friends? Or is it perhaps your grandmother?" "Yes, father. Grandmother Elona! Have you seen her? Did I miss the night's story?"

"You are right on time, my boy. She is near the water well. Go on. If you hurry, you should catch the beginning. She only just left as you arrived." Laik smiled and raced off toward the water well. He spotted her as the other children gathered around her in anticipation of the night's story. Laik squeezed into the circle as Elona spotted him and smiled.

"Tonight's story is a special one. It is a special one not because of the content or characters in the story, but because it is based on a true story." The youngsters' eyes opened wide as they continued to listen.

"Long before you were born, the haunted forest was known as the most beautiful forest that ever existed. The deer were plentiful, the trees were well-nourished and strong, and the fruits and flowers produced by these lands were enough to feed hundreds upon hundreds of villages. The dangerous and dreadful road to Anglin and their market was not needed. We were able to survive off of the fat of this forest. Its beauty was particularly of interest to the goddess of wrath. Her name was Zalia, and she was very kind, but if one ever rubbed her the wrong way, her wrath would reach unreasonable heights. Zalia's only contact with a man is the reason this forest does

6

not flourish any longer and is the reason it remains haunted to this very day."

Vidion came closer to the circle. His interest was now piqued with the thought of wrath and the haunted forest, which was forbidden to all villagers. Elona noticed his interest and continued.

"On a night like any other, a man by the name of Ghaldon decided to seek retaliation against Toewood. Ghaldon had been banned from our village because he was a well-known thief and crook. No one wanted him around, and those who knew him did not let him stay among them. Everyone knew of our beautiful forest, even Ghaldon. He scuttled into the forest and began killing deer for no reason. He also set a small tree alight, in hope that the forest would all burn, but Zalia was watching, and her rage reached heights that man had not yet witnessed. She loved life and, unless a fruit was being picked to eat, or a tree cut for shelter, she would not have it. Ghaldon was thrown to the ground, and Zalia stood over him, her eyes ablaze with anger. Even in all of her rage, Zalia allowed Ghaldon to explain himself, but the lies that flowed out of his mouth were obvious, and only angered her more. She used his face to help extinguish the flames, and the tree was saved. His face now resembled that of a monster, and his skin appeared melted."

Elona had the full attention of all the children and Vidion, who was still pretending to sharpen his sword. Some of the youngsters' parents began to feel uneasy. These were the types of stories that gave Elona the reputation of a crazy old lady who liked to tell false tales.

"As an everlasting punishment, Zalia gave Ghaldon what he desired most: power. The type of power a sorcerer or enchanter would possess. Additionally, she even granted him the opportunity to live forever, but there was a catch. His time would only revive by the taking of one's soul. He would often have to draw the life out of those who were brave enough to wander through the forest. To make things worse for Ghaldon, a curse was placed on his soul, and the only place he could survive would be within the boundaries of this forest, trapping him there forever. The forest's beauty ceased to thrive, along with the fruits and deer he took for granted. In Zalia's rage, she made sure that no man would ever be able to harm the forest she loved so much, and that no one would be able to benefit from its beauty and sustenance.

"Till this day, no one knows if he still roams the now dead, haunted forest. All that is known is that those who enter have never returned, and if you stand near enough on a well-lit night, you might catch a glimpse of what appears to be his moving shadow."

The children now looked to the right, fearfully watching for a moving shadow. Laik walked toward Vidion for comfort, while Elona made sure all of the other children returned to their homes safely.

"It's fake, you know. The story," Vidion stated.

"I don't think so, Vidion. I've seen the moving shadow myself. Honest! And why would Grandma Elona lie to us like that?" questioned Laik.

Vidion grinned, and concocted an idea of his own in his head. He knew his little brother looked up to him, and it was easy to influence him and get him to do whatever he wished for.

"You know what, Laik? You are probably right. I'm happy to have a younger brother as brave and smart as you are. Maybe we should help put the other kids' minds at ease. I'm sure they're all just as worried as you are. Let's go into the forest and find out if it's true or not." Laik's face read nothing but terror. At the same time, his older brother, who he looked up to and thought of as brave, made him hide the fear as best he could, and Laik hesitantly agreed to enter the haunted woodland. "One more thing, though, Laik. You should go alone. If our mother and father were to catch both of us in there, we would forever be grounded. If they only caught you, however, we could just tell them you went alone, and I was trying to stop you. They will punish you, but I will be able to convince them to let you out as long as you're with me." Laik thought about it for a few seconds and agreed to continue. In his mind, it made sense, but in truth, Vidion was only trying to find a way to keep his younger brother away from him.

The two brothers walked toward the forest, and felt the air getting colder and colder as they approached the outermost trees. From there, they could hear the creaks and strange noises that they had only ever been told about before now.

"Go on, Laik. If anything happens, I'll be here. Just yell," persisted Vidion, knowing full well of the dangers.

Laik trembled in fear, and the cold air did not help with the trembling. He took a step forward, and a strange heaviness began to press against his chest. It was as if something was trying to push him away from the area, but Laik ignored it and continued to push through.

"Laik!" a voice called. The boys looked back, and it was Grandma Elona. Laik walked away from the edge of the forest, and with every step he took, his chest felt lighter and lighter. "What are you boys doing?" yelled Elona.

Vidion thought quickly and responded with what sounded like pure sincerity. "Grandma! He was trying to go into the forest! He wanted to see if your story was true for himself. I tried to stop him, but he wouldn't listen! So I chased him as he ran away from me. It was only at the edge where he finally stopped, and I was just trying to talk some sense into him. Don't be mad at him, Grandma. Don't be mad. I'm sure he has a reason."

Laik was now on the stage. He remembered the agreement between him and his brother and did not wish to get him into trouble. Laik expressed how sorry he was and that he had only done it to calm his friends, who were petrified. Elona heaved a sigh of relief and hugged her youngest grandson.

"It's okay, Laik. It's okay. But going forward, speak to me. Listen to your older brother. People who enter this forest truly disappear. I would hate to never be able to see you again. Now, both of you, come. It's time for bed, and you know how strict Grandpa Otto is about bedtime. He turns into a grouch if he doesn't get his sleep."

The following morning, Laik, Vidion, their father, and grand-parents woke up peacefully to the smell of freshly baked bread. They were met with all of the flavored jellies one could think of, a warm apple pie, the richest of butters, and freshly cut bacon, to name but a few things. Once all were attended to, Myla happily took her seat, and they all began to eat. Myla and Quinn snickered at each other and whispered in secret until they finally decided that Quinn would speak. Vidion chewed his food, and became annoyed, as he prepared to listen to what he thought would be his chore for the day.

"Good morning to you all once again. I hope you are all enjoying the delicious foods your mother has cooked for us." They all listened while they continued to stuff their faces relentlessly. "I have news to share with you all, and it's news that will surely bring joy to our village and especially our home." Vidion slowed his chewing, his mouth full of bread, and listened carefully. Deep down, he knew what it was going to be, but hoped that he was wrong. "Myla and I are having another baby! Vidion. Laik. You are going to have a baby brother or sister!" Laik jumped for joy and hugged his mother and father in excitement. Vidion forced a smile and congratulated them, but was screaming inside. He hated his family and could only think of a newborn as yet another person who would replace him. After a short while, he excused himself from breakfast and went to the washroom. The rest of his family spoke about all of the changes and fun the new baby would bring.

Almost before they knew it, the baby had arrived. It was again a boy, and they named him Iolas.

After a few months of recovery, Quinn and Myla continued with their village duties. All residents of Toewood were responsible for something that helped them live or grow as a village. Quinn and Myla had the most dangerous task of bringing back goods from the bazaar. While it did not sound terrible, what made it a treacherous journey was the fact that there was only one way to the bazaar. It was over the mountain and over a perilous bridge. Crossing an old wooden bridge with the weight of the carriage, goods, and horses was no safe or easy task.

On a day like any other, the two kissed their boys goodnight and prepared for the night's trek toward the bazaar. They usually left at bedtime so that they would arrive by the early morning. Both would take shifts sleeping and guiding the horses. It was the only way they would make it there on time and return in a speedy manner. Laik watched them through the window as the lanterns from their carriage disappeared into the night. A strange gut-wrenching feeling twisted his stomach. It was a feeling that told him to go with them, but before leaving, his parents had asked him to help Elona and

Otto with Iolas. Elona and Otto were the eldest of the village and were considered the village leaders. Vidion, on the other hand, was left with the task of collecting firewood for the town. It was unusually cold for the time of the year, and firewood would be a necessity.

The following morning, Laik opened his eyes after a long night, during which he had slept well. He once again looked out of the window, knowing that his parents would not return for another day or two, but thought he would check anyway. What he did see was that the entire village was draped in ankle-deep snow, and most of the villagers were still in their homes enjoying the warmth of a fire.

As usual, Vidion was nowhere to be found, and the rest of the household lay sound asleep. Laik quietly started a fire in the fireplace to help keep his grandparents and baby brother warm and dressed himself to go outside to play with his friends. His once overly-long cloak now fit him just right and no longer dragged on the floor as he walked. On the porch, an eerie feeling settled in his chest. The sound of the wind and the ice-cold breeze on his face felt troubling. In the distance, someone approached the village from the front gates, but he did not dare approach the figure because he did not recognize him. The traveler reached the first cabin and knocked insistently. It seemed as though he was in dire need of help. A few words were exchanged between the two, and Laik's neighbor quickly ran in for his coat, only to come rushing straight back out and toward him.

"Laik! Where is Elona? Where is Otto?" he demanded, and it was perhaps at this very moment that Laik first began to fear death. His heart sank to the pit of his stomach, and his tongue was unable to form a word. Deep down inside, he knew what the urgency was about.

Otto grabbed his coat and ran outside. After a few moments, he jumped on his horse and headed in the direction the traveler had come from. There were no words or explanations for his family, but the urgency was clear from the haste he was in. Shortly before supper, he returned with a dead stare on his face. He took a seat at the dinner table as Elona grabbed and hung his coat. His skin was frostbitten, but not an ounce of pain did he show. Otto appeared dead inside. Vidion was serving himself a bowl of stew as he watched his grandfather sit in complete silence. As Elona and Laik tried to comfort him and get a word or two out of him, Vidion poked fun at them in his head. He thought of them as weak and pathetic for letting something bother them so much.

Otto inhaled and exhaled deeply. As he swallowed his saliva, his gulp seemed to go down as if he were trying to eat a rock. His eyes began to water, and he finally mustered the strength to look his grandchildren and his wife in the eyes.

"Our Myla and Quinn. They were headed to the market," he managed to spit out. "They were headed to the market, and the weather caught them. It was cold last night. Windy. It snowed hard." He paused and looked at Elona again; this time, his eyes were very watery. "They seem to have reached the bridge, but I don't know. Maybe they couldn't see. It was dark, cold, and windy. The snow was thick."

Elona took a deep breath. She knew deep down inside that she had lost her daughter Myla and her son-in-law, Quinn, but what hurt her most was that she knew her grandchildren had lost their parents. Shortly after Elona exhaled, Otto confirmed that their bodies had been found at the bottom of the cliff, along with the horses and carriage. They never made it to the bazaar, and the bridge seemed to have collapsed under them. Although she was saddened, Elona could not help but also feel great resentment toward King Nevil, who was a tyrant at best. For years, Elona had written to him in hope of gaining safer access to the market or for permission to build a closer one. However, the king's response was always a no.

Laik sat on a stool he'd once helped his father make. It was one of his fondest memories, because it was the first time he'd successfully made something with his father's guidance. The idea of death submerged his thoughts as question after question soon piled up in his mind. What happens when you die? Where do you go? When will I die? Does it hurt? Are the gods real? Why do they allow us to suffer?

Question after question and thought after thought kept the tears from running down his pale skin, but inside he was screaming. He would never again get the chance to hunt with his father or learn how to forge his own swords. He would never again get to hug his mother and listen to her soft voice tell him she loved him. His world was at an end, yet on the other side of the room, Vidion watched his family coolly as they internally crumbled to pieces. He seemed to be emotionless and unaffected by the death of his mother. Laik wiped the tears from his eyes, not knowing what he could do to feel better. At the sight of his older brother, his eyes began to water once more as he walked toward him for comfort. Vidion stood still as his younger brother hugged him, making sure his grandparents didn't witness the lack of affection. It was almost as if Vidion was elated to hear about the news of his parents' death. Their sorrows were briefly distracted by a sudden knock. They walked toward the door, and two of their neighbors had come to give their condolences.

The news of Myla's and Quinn's deaths quickly spread throughout the village, and one by one, the villagers lit a candle in their honor. Before they knew it, Elona and Otto found themselves at the burial. Laik stood behind them, observing. Most of the villagers were saddened, their heads lowered. The drops of rain trickled down their faces and off their noses. His grandparents stood near the stones that were carefully placed over the bodies, as a prayer was said for their souls. Laik was hurt, and shocked at the sight of their bodies. It was the first time Laik had seen a dead body, and the fact that these were his mother and father did not help at all.

Elona and Otto tried to remain strong for Laik, knowing their tears would only scare him more, but Laik knew that they were holding back. He looked around for his older brother, to seek comfort from him. After a few minutes of gazing through the crowd of people paying their respects, he spotted Vidion sitting under a tree far behind the gathering. Laik walked toward his older brother, kissing his baby brother Iolas on the cheek as he passed; a family friend was holding him during this difficult time for his family.

"I don't know what to do, Vidion. I want to cry, but I can't. I want to say it will all be okay, but how do I know that they are okay? How do I know they are now at peace with the gods, smiling down on us like all of Grandma's stories say?" Irritated, Vidion looked at Laik and smirked. He stretched his arms up in the air and asked for him to sit down next to him.

"I can tell you what I think, but you probably wouldn't want to hear it. Maybe I shouldn't."

Desperate for answers, Laik begged for his words. He hoped that Vidion would have the answers he sought for. After all, to Laik, he was his older and wiser brother.

"Please, Vidion. Please. I want to know the truth. I want to put my mind at ease, and I want to know that our mother and father are resting in peace." Vidion smirked once again and replied.

"Well, I must first add that Quinn was not my father, and both of them probably deserved it." Laik's heart sank.

"Why would you say that, Vidion? They loved us. They loved our village. They didn't deserve to die."

"I'm sorry, Laik. I didn't mean to say that," he said with the least sincerity Laik had ever heard. It was Vidion's hatred toward them that had slipped out. The only reason he apologized was because he did not want Laik to tell their grandparents.

"Look... I can tell you what I think, but you have to promise not to tell Elona or Otto. As you can see, they are grieving, and you wouldn't want to make them feel worse, would you?" Laik hesitantly agreed, a bit uneasy at the fact that his brother felt their parents deserved to die. Still, Laik listened with the hope that there was some sort of answer his brother could provide.

"I promise. I won't say a word."

"Okay. Well, think about it. I can only see two possible outcomes. One, the stories about the gods must be untrue. If they existed, why would they allow bad things to happen to good people? If they existed, why did this happen?" Laik paused for a second and thought about it. For a moment, he thought that Vidion had made a valid point, but Laik recalled what Elona had told him about the gods.

"...Because they do everything for a reason."

"And what fit reason do you see that your parents had to die? What good did that bring? It can only mean one other thing, Laik; outcome number two. It means that the gods do not care about us." Laik remained silent as his eyes began to water. He had nothing to say and no retort to give because, in his mind, Vidion had made his point. He thought about his parents and the nothingness that was now their existence. Was life nothing but an empty void, a void that even he was headed to one day? He took a seat under the tree as his brother walked away. The morning became sundown, and sundown became night as he sat there quietly thinking about life and death. Uncertainties filled his thoughts until the only certainty became the fact that his parents were no longer there.

2

A Safe Passage

A cool breeze rustled through the leaves, the sound of it soothing. Laik peacefully woke up, realizing that he had fallen asleep under the tree while dwelling on his thoughts. Otto had seen him fast asleep as the burial came to an end and felt it would be best to let him rest. It had been two days since Laik had gotten a good night's sleep.

He had finally awoken the morning after the funeral ceremony, his honey-colored eyes sealed shut with a thick lining of what he and his friends called eye boogers. After a few bites of an apple that fell from the tree, Laik headed home to find his grandparents in a dispute. It was odd for them to argue because they usually worked things out peacefully and were very understanding of one another.

"What's going on, Grandma?" asked Laik, praying that everything at the funeral had gone well. Placing Iolas on a patch of soft hay as he continued with his nap, Otto responded for Elona. "My boy, I am sorry. We don't mean to frighten you. It's just that your grandmother has the crazy idea of marching into King Nevil's lair and demanding either that the passage to the bazaar be made safe, and easy to travel, or that a new one be made altogether."

Naturally, this concerned everyone, not only Otto and Laik, but all of Toewood as well. King Nevil was the sort of ruler who would behead a beggar for stealing a slice of bread. It was a well-known fact that Elona's father had spent the last days of his life imprisoned because of the mere fact that he did not bow fast enough in the king's presence. The villagers of Toewood unsurprisingly worried that passage to the market would be sealed or, worse yet, all of the villagers would be killed or imprisoned for Elona's demands. Nonetheless, Elona trekked her way to the king for nearly four days, and finally found herself at an inn near his castle. The kingdom had just finished celebrating King Nevil's eighty-seventh birthday, which was the only time of the year that he was in a somewhat generous mood.

The following morning, Elona walked toward the front gates. The closer she got, the faster her heart beat, as though it wanted to jump out of her chest, but she refused to show it. The locals all looked at her with a face that asked what in the world she was doing. Moments later, Elona reached the first set of guards, who instantly blocked her way.

"Halt! What business does a beggar, much less a woman, have here at this hour?" Elona took a deep breath, well aware of the fact that this was usually the position of a man. The king detested speaking to women about business, politics, or anything other than himself and sex.

"The king. He has requested to see me. About an important matter in the village of Toewood." The two guards looked at each other and laughed, knowing full well that King Nevil did not speak to women.

"Go on, lady. Get out of here. Go back to the hole you call a home. The King requested no such thing. Spare yourself and walk away. You know very well that he would have your head for this." Elona paused and thought for a second, making sure that the next words out of her mouth sounded bold, yet convincing.

"Yes. I know that very well, indeed. But it seems as if the two of you are not as keen as you are daring, hiding behind your armor, weapons, and the knowledge that if anyone were to touch you or speak to you the wrong way... they are as good as dead. Talking back to you would almost be the equivalent to speaking to the king himself in this way. Would you not agree?" The two knights looked at each other, their blood boiling from the disrespect they received from Elona.

"You old hag! I should hang you myself. Get yourself out of here before I throw you out myself." Elona looked at them dead in the eye and finally smiled before continuing.

"Look at me, lads. Look at me...would I, a peasant, filth even, really march down here with this level of confidence and demand to see the king if what I were saying were false? I am very aware that he would have my head for this if I were lying, but one has to wonder, as one of his men, what happens if you defy him? What happens if you refuse access to one of his requested guests? What would he do to the both of you if you do not let his invited guest in?" The two soldiers paused and looked at one another, wondering now if her words were true. Although they had not received word about any visitors, King Nevil was known to be forgetful and often forgot to inform his men on similar matters.

The two guards hesitantly escorted Elona through the castle and straight to the doors of the great hall. On the other side of the room, King Nevil sat on his throne, discussing a dispute that was going on with the kingdom closest to them. Their king was named Theros, and the two had long disputed over a piece of land. It was right in the middle of both of their borders. Both Nevil and Theros were greedy and did not wish to give up half of the land to the other. They both wanted it all, because its soil was rich, and its harvest was plentiful. Additionally, there lay within the land a mountain, which had not yet been explored. It was believed to possess a plethora of jewels and riches.

The guards walked fearfully away and let the knights inside of the hall handle whatever was to come. Elona forced open the massive doors to the great hall and walked toward King Nevil. The entire room grew silent. Each of Elona's footsteps now echoed as the distance between her and the king shortened. King Nevil watched as she approached the steps to his throne, each footstep angering him. He wondered what this woman was doing in his hall and why she was interrupting a meeting between two kings.

"Good day, King Nevil," Elona exclaimed while hiding the fact that she was trembling in fear. "I apologize for the sudden intrusion, but I have a situation that must be attended to as soon as possible." Elona knelt and bowed her head while she awaited the king's response. The king looked at his guards for answers, but the answers did not come. None of them knew who she was or how she got in. The king now grew embarrassed at the fact that King Theros had witnessed how poorly his knights guarded the premises and how he was rudely disrespected and interrupted by a peasant. Not knowing how to handle the situation, since this was the first time it had happened, he decided to allow her to speak.

"Well, go on, woman. What is it that you want?" Elona

swallowed her saliva as if she were trying to swallow a mouth full of bread without chewing. She realized that she had unintentionally made the king look bad in front of the gathering and, worse than that, in front of his royal rival.

"My lord, my name is Elona, and I am responsible for making sure that the day-to-day life and duties of Toewood run smoothly. Once again, I wish to apologize for coming in unannounced. I know of your ruthless, yet great, leadership, and I know very well that I risk my life by doing this." Elona paused for a moment, knowing that the only way out of this would be by making him sound like a respected, powerful tyrant of a King. "When I was a young girl, you imprisoned my father because he did not show you the respect you desired fast enough. I never got to see him again, and I grew up without a father. I have heard of the stories where people have lost their hands for pocketing a piece of fruit. I truly and personally know of the consequences. I tell you this so that you may consider the fact that I have come all this way to make a request, even knowing how unforgiving you can be."

King Nevil listened and watched, while Theros seemed to appear uneasy after hearing of his ruthlessness. Elona planned to instill fear in Theros, since it would likely change King Nevil's opinion of her, and it seemed to have worked. Nevil allowed Elona to continue in the hope that King Theros would begin thinking twice about defying him. Elona continued.

"The nearest market to Toewood is a long and treacherous journey. The only way to make it there quickly is on foot, without a carriage. Still, the carriage, as you surely know, is necessary to bring back large amounts of food for our people. The issue is that there is only one passage to the market. That passage is unforgiving, especially during the cold months when it snows. The passage has a very narrow channel, which is not meant for carriages to pass through. The only other way is to travel around the other side of the mountain, which would take nearly seven days. Three times have our people gone for food and supplies and never returned. Two days ago, my only daughter and her husband went and lost their lives. They left behind three beautiful boys, which my husband and I are now taking care of in full." Elona stopped once again; this time to hold back her tears and urge to raise her voice at the King. "I had to bury my child and the love of her life. I had to bury them while their children stood there watching... and the only thing I could tell them was that it was going to be okay. I had to tell them that they were now at peace... but what do we know about peace and the afterlife?" Elona added the rhetorical question knowing that most people did not believe in the gods. She was a huge believer and often shared stories about them with the children of Toewood, in hope of spreading the belief of their existence.

King Nevil continued to listen. It was Elona's great fortune that he was indeed in a good mood, and her words had frightened King Theros. Usually, someone behaving like this would have their tongue wrenched out, and never have the ability to speak again. Theros continued to listen carefully; his entire body now turned toward the conversation in full mindfulness. It was clear that he was now worried about his own life.

"So I come to you, sire, not for pity and not for compassion, but for a mutual benefit. We need a safer passage to the market. Providing us with that would, in turn, benefit you because more people will quickly and safely travel to the bazaar and spend money. The taxes go to you, King Nevil. An entire village, and the villages south of us, will more frequently be spending money which you will benefit from."

The King thought for a minute and looked at Theros. Theros' full attention was on the King, and it was a crucial moment for Theros to witness.

"In all my years as King of Asplin, not one person has ever approached me the way you have. To begin with, you barge in here as if you own the place and interrupt a crucial meeting. However, you come not only with a problem you want me to solve but also with a suggestion, which, as you say, has a 'mutual benefit'. Usually, I would have you strung up on a rope by now, but you thought about me. You thought about my interest and my well-being, as well. As a reward, I will permit you to build a passage through the mountains. My men will provide you with the explosives you need to get through the base of the high land, but you will be responsible for the rest. As for your punishment..."

Elona froze. She held her breath as she awaited her fate. Would she be tortured? Executed? Or would she have her tongue ripped out? The king pondered for a few seconds and continued.

"Your village will be charged double the tax for your intrusion. Be aware that I spare your life because you thought of mine. However, if anyone from Toewood believes this kind of behavior is acceptable, and tries it again, their heads will be mounted on a pole. This includes you. My floors were cleaned only yesterday, so please, leave. Your stench and dirty clothing has brought filth to my home."

Elona once again bowed her head to show her gratitude. As she walked out of the hall, the king barked an order to his knights. "Ensure that this Elona leaves the premises at once. Escort her to her town and beat her. Do not kill her, but leave her with enough markings for her people to see. As promised, have a few of our men deliver the explosives to Toewood, but do not help them with the passage. My knights will not be partaking in slave work."

The knights followed Elona closely back to Toewood with a carriage filled with explosives. From time to time, Elona looked back, making sure they were still behind her, just as she used to do for her grandchildren when they were toddlers. The thought of being beaten never crossed her mind, even though the guards were mocking her the whole way home. Elona was a bit on the heavy side, and the guards teased her with the sounds of cows and pigs. Naturally, this crushed Elona. Her self-esteem was already low because she was old, and the villagers all called her crazy. With every oink and moo, her eyes watered, but she hid her embarrassment with every ounce of strength that she had.

Toewood was now in sight, and Elona advised the guards. They all looked ahead at the village, which was quiet. All of the villagers were still in their homes, making breakfast, and the smoke from their chimney rose high into the air.

"Stop!" shouted the commander. The fourteen knights came to a halt and awaited instruction, all of them knowing that Elona would now be beaten. It was only then that Elona looked at the commander's face and realized who it was. It was the guard she had tricked and made a fool of. "As ordered by King Nevil, we will deliver the package to your village. The package will be left on the opposite end of the narrow passage, where you and your people will have to figure out a way to safely get it over to your side. Further orders are to punish you as a message to Toewood. None of you will ever dare march into the castle as you have, Elona. We are also responsible for punishing the village leaders of all villages near you. No one will get the idea that what you did was acceptable. Now... without further delay, your punishment will proceed."

Elona closed her eyes and mentally accepted her fate. The knights backhanded her and pushed her to the ground, her left eye swelling shut almost immediately. On the left side of her forehead, an abrasion bled and trickled down her face, mixing with the tears of pain. As she tried to stand, she could taste the blood in her mouth from several teeth that had been knocked out of their sockets. The men laughed at her misfortune, though they were careful not to kill her as ordered. At long last, the commander allowed her to stand and spoke to her.

"I'll have you know that I will likely work graveyard hours because of you. Nothing has brought me more pleasure in all of my years of service than this moment. I hope you learn never to cross King Nevil's men, but more importantly, never to cross me, you fat bitch!" And before she knew it, the commander struck her in the nose with his staff, breaking her nose and watched her drop to the cold, wet ground. Elona stayed there as the men unloaded the carriage and rode toward the next village.

Shortly after sunset, Elona managed to hobble her way back home. One of the villagers saw her from a distance and quickly helped her the rest of the way home. Otto bathed her and aided her as best as he could, while Vidion stood back and laughed at the whole ordeal. Laik, on the other hand, watched and listened in horror as Elona explained what had happened from start to finish. After she was finally at rest in her bed with a cup of hot tea by the warm fire, he approached her slowly. Vidion continued to watch and listen.

"Grandma... are you going to die?" questioned Laik. Elona started to laugh. Not because she thought it was funny, but because she wanted him to feel like everything was going to be okay.

"I am not going to die, my boy. All of the swelling will go down. This will all go away. I promise."

"But what happened? How did you end up like this? The people are saying that someone beat you and left you in a puddle of your own blood." Elona looked over at Otto, who seemed to be catching a terrible cold.

Otto interrupted, "My boy... yes. It is true. As punishment for entering the great hall, the knights were ordered to beat her, but it's okay. Your grandmother will recover and be on her feet in no time. Now let's leave her to rest while we eat our supper. I made a huge pot of chicken soup for us to enjoy on this cold, cold night."

Elona shut her eyes for what felt like several hours. In reality, it had not even passed one hour when she woke to find Laik sitting on a stool right beside her. She smiled and made herself comfortable before speaking. "You can't sit here all night, you know. I promise I'm okay, Laik. I will be up on my feet by morning." Laik smiled and hesitated to ask a question. Elona sensed it, and playfully demanded to know what was on his mind. He forced a smile and spoke. Vidion still listened carefully as their voices wafted through the house.

"Are you sure you're not going to die, Grandma?" Elona once again laughed to make him feel better.

"I am not going to die, my boy. I will be fine in the morning. I promise." Laik still had a look of concern on his face, because that was not exactly what he had meant.

"I meant...ever, Grandma. Are you ever going to die? Or will you be here forever?" Elona sighed and sat up. It was a difficult subject that she was not prepared for, and it was not easy to tell a twelve-year-old that she would one day pass on, especially a twelve-year-old who had just lost his parents.

27

"Laik... I will, my boy. One day I will pass away, but it won't be for many, many years. You will be an old man." Laik smiled and hugged his grandmother.

"I love you, Grandma."

It made him feel slightly more at peace, but he still wondered and had to ask. He asked Elona about the afterlife and the heavens. He always heard people speak of the heavens and how people go there when they die but never spoke to anyone about it. It was confusing to him, because it was odd to believe that people walked around above the clouds. Elona sat up and prepared to tell her grandson about how the gods came to be. She figured it would make him feel better when he learned that even the gods once roamed these very lands.

"Eons ago, children ran from village to village unattended, and the elders had no concern for rape, murder, theft, or even death. Death came to all with an ease of mind, because they knew that an afterlife awaited them. People believed in the good of the gods, and the gods believed in the good of the people. One could even say that it was a perfect world. Many of our neighbors today believe this story to be untrue, but I can assure you that it did occur.

"It was easy to believe in the gods back then, because they roamed the planet with us. The first gods to exist, who created everything we know, were a group of five brothers, and each of them had a specific power that made him unique. The oldest was named Knilan. He was the god of knowledge, and people would sail the deepest of seas to seek his guidance. It was said that he was never proven wrong. His predictions and his counsel never failed, and his skills with a sword were impeccable. This was, of course, because he invented the blade and mastered the craft.

28

"Next in age was Airos. He provided us with the wind for our sails and the air that fills our lungs. It was also said that he was able to change the course of a storm. People would often watch him as he spread pollen and seed throughout the land. He worked closely with Erthos, his younger brother, who planted the seeds. From them, the most beautiful and exotic flowers would bloom, and trees would spread like wildfire across the land. The trees would often form forests, some of which we still roam today. Fruits, nuts, and vegetables were gifts from Erthos to the people, and the valleys and mountains too. Rumor has it that Erthos was so strong that he would shift mountains aside the way a man would move a rock.

"Then there was Flonius. Flonius was empowered with the element of fire. He provided us with the light that guides us through the night and the warmth we have on cold evenings like this one. Although he had a good heart, he was perhaps the most ill-tempered of the brothers, but the youngest of the five was always there to keep him calm; Wyolus. He was the god of water and formed every river, ocean, and lake we bathe in. Tears of the sky would crash against the soil, which quenched all that was green and alive. The mere sight of this would mesmerize Flonius and would calm him whenever his temper got the best of him. The five brothers created a balance in our world, and a balance with each other. One helped tame the other and provided guidance if his actions were wrong. In the eyes of the people, they were perfect, but even the gods had their struggles. Love was something that was created by people, and not even Knilan was able to see past it. Love is blind, and that meant not being able to see one's faults.

"He fell head over heels in love with a lassie named Syn. Everything he did was for her. On the nights she felt warm,

29

Knilan would convince Airos to cool things down. Whenever Knilan wished to drink with his brothers, she would sway his thoughts into staying with her. Syn was boundless with her ability to manipulate, and she only cared about what she wanted. It was a trait she had learned from her mother.

"Everything was always about her. Syn became so good at getting what she wanted that the villagers began to grow upset. The things she wanted were usually granted to her because of her way with words. Syn was so good with them that she was able to convince Knilan he was wrong even if he were right. Since Knilan was a god, it was effortless for her to get what she wanted through him, but one night the villagers had had enough. Syn had convinced Knilan to cover the sun for four days. She claimed her reason was to make sure the people received plentiful rest after months of hard labor. In reality, her intentions stemmed from jealousy. She was jealous of the fact that people loved Knilan; she was jealous of the fact that people sought after him, and most of all, she was jealous of any woman who dared share a word with him.

"During the four days of no sun, the crops froze over, and all the hard labor went to waste. Some of the villagers began to freeze to death. Syn, Knilan, and his brothers were safe and warm in a cabin deep in the woods. They stayed there to celebrate Syn's birthday, and all the while, the brothers remained oblivious to the fact that the world around them was crumbling. Upon returning to the village on the fifth day, once the sun had returned, the strong ones who had survived the cold gathered their strength. They figured the only explanation for the sun's absence had something to do with the gods, and it was confirmed by none other than Syn.

"Syn betrayed Knilan and the other brothers. She tricked the villagers into thinking that she was kidnapped and beaten by the five of them. In a fit of rage, the villagers quickly gathered their weapons and vowed to kill the gods for mistreating one of their own and, more importantly, a woman. Under the command of Syn, the men hunted for the gods day and night, but word got to the five brothers rather quickly. Their heads were wanted at the end of a spear, but more than that, Syn wanted The Bloodstone. It was the sword of Knilan, but what made it unique was its mesmerizing power. The sword could withstand any blade it clashed against, and what made it even more rare was the fact that it was made from a tree that no longer existed. The tree was known for its durability and uniquely shaped leaves. It was the staple Syn needed to become Queen, and it was all she truly ever wanted from Knilan; power.

"After days of running and hiding, the brothers finally came to a realization. They had the power to easily stop them all, but it would mean they would have to slay. Killing hundreds of innocent people was not their way. They realized that if they killed Syn herself, it would only increase the fury of the villagers. The brothers would be on the run forever, with no one to believe them. The only way to put an end to it all for good would be to leave the world they had created and watch over from the clouds above. Knilan imbedded The Bloodstone into the grounds of the eastern forest, and the other four circled it. The spirits of Airos, Flonius, Wyolus, and Erthos were transferred into The Bloodstone, forming a storm like no other. Their powers were now in the sword.

"At that moment, the villagers felt the strong winds from the east and darted toward the storm. Knilan quickly grabbed The Bloodstone and fled to The Lost Island, an island he and his brothers had created. No one knew of this island because it was located deep within the mist of a large, great lake. The waters were infested with creatures unknown to man, and no one dared enter the lake out of fear. There, on The Lost Island, in a cavern, Knilan hid The Bloodstone and ensured that no man would ever lay their hands on its great power; the power of the gods. The villagers never found the bodies of the four brothers, and Knilan eventually returned in secret and burned their bodies to ash."

Laik sat mesmerized by the tale and, at the same time, felt better knowing the story of the gods. It suddenly made sense to him. There was a reason why they did not walk among them any longer, and it comforted him to know that his parents were safely in the care of the gods. Still, he was curious and couldn't help but wonder about the tree.

"Grandma, the tree. Why does it not exist any longer?" asked Laik.

"That is a story for another day, my boy," responded Elona with a smile.

Laik tucked himself into bed after kissing Elona goodnight. He blew the candles out and looked over at Vidion's bed to wish him goodnight, but his older brother sat on the edge of his bed wide awake. Vidion quietly scooted over to him and began to whisper.

"You know that you are my little brother and I love you. I do not doubt that you know that... and because I care about you so much, I wanted to tell you the truth about the story Grandma just told you." Laik's heart sank. He knew deep down inside that it would not be something he liked, but it was something he had to know.

"Tell me. Please. Are Mom and Dad really at peace in the clouds with them?" Vidion lowered his head and pretended to sympathize, shaking his head no and forcing his eyes to water as if he cared.

"I'm afraid not, Laik. That's what I wanted to tell you. You see... the story Grandma just mentioned is a story that is told to people who cannot cope with death that easily. It is meant to help you feel at ease when a loved one dies or when you are on your deathbed. The truth is... like I mentioned before, the gods do not exist." Laik became saddened at the thought of non-existence, as it triggered a fear inside of him that he could not express. He tried to catch his breath, but it was as if his lungs were unable to take in the air around him. "Look at Grandpa, for instance," Vidion continued. "If you have been watching closely as I have, he is getting very sick. He has been coughing a storm, and it has not gotten any better. Before you know it, he will begin coughing blood and will be buried just like our parents. I've seen it before. Remember, Laik, if the gods did exist, there would be no sickness or death. There would be nothing to worry about, but here you are, worried."

Vidion sarcastically wished him a goodnight and went to bed with a smile. His younger brother barely slept that night because of the thoughts that thundered through his mind. His chest was tight with a pressure that felt strong enough to crush a boulder, and his eyes stayed open until his brain practically shut down just before the sunrise. Elona had awoken to begin preparing breakfast, and Vidion, who was well rested, purposefully made a ruckus to awaken Laik. Vidion and Laik tottered to the table while Elona finished up, and just before Laik rested his head on the wooden table, Elona turned to speak to them. "Good morning, my boys. I need a favor from the both of you."

33

3

The Five Brothers of Toewood

Both Elona and Otto had always been independent. They worked their entire lives, beginning as soon as they were able to follow an order, but age was the one thing that eventually slowed them down. Time is something that everyone and everything runs out of. The boys listened carefully to their grandmother's request, Laik groggy, and his eyes reddish and stinging. Elona asked for the boys to run errands at the market going forward. The older villagers would take turns with the horse and carriage, while others worked on creating a safer path through the mountains. After the tiring walk to King Nevil's hall and the fact that Otto was clearly getting sick, she realized that the days of heavy travel for them were over. Their knees, hips, and other joints were practically wasted from old age, and Otto found himself bedridden for much of the day.

Vidion hated going to the market because it meant he had to interact with others. He hated people, but what he hated most was the fact that he now had to frequent the area with his younger brother. Even more than that, it meant he had to speak with Laik as they traveled. The two siblings finally reached the shops when Laik began to talk to him about their grandfather.

"Do you think Grandpa is going to be okay? I know it's only been a few days, but it seems as if he is only getting worse. I worry for him, Vidion. You know... since he's old and all." Vidion rolled his eyes and responded.

"As long as you don't see him cough blood, I think he will be all right. Coughing blood is a sure sign of death, but he is a strong man. Don't you think?" Laik nodded his head up and down. Otto and his father, Quinn, were the two strongest men in the world in his mind, and to be fair, they were indeed tough men.

Vidion and Laik finally reached the shops where the most delicious breads were baked and purchased two loaves as requested. Vidion also managed to sneak a few extra pieces into his bag and walk away without anyone noticing; or so he thought.

"Psst..." a voice called from an alley. Vidion figured it was for someone else and continued walking. "Psst!" he heard again, but this time Laik noticed and advised his brother. Frustrated and annoyed, Vidion turned toward the alley, and a beggar in a dull old cloak called at them. It was strange for a beggar to ask for anything other than money, especially since it was common for them to get beaten. No one wanted them wandering their streets, and no one wanted them near the shops for the simple fact that they were the main ones responsible for theft.

The beggar introduced himself as Olec and unbeknownst to them, he was a beggar who was seeking a way to save himself from the dark sorcerer that lurked in the haunted forest. "Forgive me for my intrusion, but I promise my words will be worth your while. I don't have the intention to ask for money, and I don't have the intention to ask for a piece of the bread that you stole, Vidion." The brothers were dumbfounded. Laik looked at his older brother and wondered why he had stolen. He'd always looked up to him and considered him a role model, even though Vidion had always belittled him. Vidion, on the other hand, remained curious to know how Olec knew of his name.

"How do you know my name? Who are you?"

"I told you. I am Olec, and I just so happened to overhear the conversation you had with your little brother. What if I were to tell you that I know of a way to cure your grandfather?"

"Go away, old man, before I slit your throat," he replied. Olec smirked, took two steps toward Vidion with his cane, and whispered,

"Tell the little one to step away. There is something in this for you too." Vidion thought for a moment and forced his little brother to wait outside of the alley. He was now intrigued because there might be something to gain out of this.

"I know more about you than you think, Vidion. I wouldn't attempt to make a proposition with you if there wasn't a mutual benefit. Why would you be interested in it if there was nothing in it for you? You see, a few years back, I became curious about the stories that are said about the haunted forest. I entered the forest, thinking that it couldn't be true, but I hoped that they were. I would have given anything to become higher than the people I lived among. Deep inside those hidden woodlands, I saw the shadow myself. I found the stories were indeed true, for I suddenly found my life at the mercy of Ghaldon himself. I begged for my life. I begged like a dog, but none of it seemed to matter to him until I remembered the tales. His only way to immortality was through the souls of those who wandered through his lands. Still, after ages of people disappearing, it became difficult to obtain them. So I offered my eternal service to him in exchange for my soul. I promised him that I would bring him people, to feed on." Vidion became impatient, wondering what this had to do with him, and urged the old man to get to the point. The old man took another few steps toward him, and Vidion could smell the stench of garbage and feces on his clothes.

"If Ghaldon had it his way, he would consume the souls of the most wicked folks in our lands. The fouler the person, the stronger he becomes. You, Vidion, happen to be the most immoral person he can see, but you have never entered his domain. He can sense it, and he has told me all about you. I know you do not care for a cure, but you do thirst for control. You thirst for power. You want people to fear you."

Vidion's attention was now piqued as he looked back to make sure his brother was still away.

"Go on, old man. You have my interest."

"You seek power while I seek freedom. I am a slave to Ghaldon, and now that I know what it feels like to have my freedom taken away from me, freedom is the only thing I want! So I bring you this... Ghaldon tells me of a place where the ashes of the four gods rest. He tells me that before Knilan left for the heavens, he gave his brothers their final resting place. The place is called The Grayfalls, gray because of the thick layer of fog that engulfs it. Ghaldon claims that the ashes are powerful enough to end his curse. If you manage to get your hands on these ashes, he will release me and give you the ability to heal. You will become the most powerful healer to ever exist! I am too old and frail for such a task, to be honest, which is why I don't do it myself. You are going to need someone small, someone like your brother. There are cracks and crevices that even you won't fit through." Vidion thought in silence for a moment and considered the possibility of becoming a powerful healer. He was not particularly interested in becoming a healer, but his thoughts were soon interrupted by Olec's devious persistence.

"You have nothing to lose, Vidion. If I'm lying, all you lose is a few hours of sleep. You will probably find me one day and beat me to death. If I'm not, then I will be free, you will become mighty, and Ghaldon will have what he needs to become more powerful than the gods ever were."

Olec emphasized that if Vidion were to take this quest, it would have to be done before the next full moon. In reality, the full moon had nothing to do with any of it. Still, Olec knew that at the end of the day, Vidion would believe anything if it meant he could be anywhere near as mighty as a sorcerer. He handed him a map of where the ashes were, and with that, Vidion was on his way. Laik began to ask his older brother questions about the beggar. Although Vidion felt bothered by his brother's curiosity, he tried to calm his temper. Vidion knew he would need him, as advised by Olec. He was the only person small enough that he would be able to trick into going with him, and that he did. He told Laik that the old man offered a cure for Otto and the chance for Elona to live forever. This, of course, piqued Laik's attention, because the one thing on his mind was death; the death of his family, the end of his friends, and the death of himself.

"Think about it, my little brother. I want to be honest with you. It is a perilous journey, and I don't know what is going to happen, but if we are successful, none of us will ever have to worry about death. We get to live forever, old man Olec will be free, and you and I will no longer worry. Now go play with your friends and think about it. Do not tell anyone, though,

Laik. You never know. Someone might want to steal the ashes for themselves, for other reasons." Vidion planted the seed in Laik's mind very carefully and was mindful not to reveal his true intentions. While he intended indeed to retrieve the ashes to become a powerful healer, he also had other things in mind. He thought if the ashes were all Ghaldon needed to become more powerful than the gods, why not keep the ashes for himself? Why not let Ghaldon concoct the potion and take it from him? These were all questions that his greed wanted to make a reality.

After Laik disappeared with his friends, Vidion quietly snuck into his bed and began to analyze the map. Elona and the village healer were at the dinner table speaking about Otto and his health. Iolas slept in his grandmother's arms while they talked. The healer was unable to determine what the cause of Otto's illness was but suspected that it was something that would eventually take him to the grave. Vidion looked over at his grandfather and, on the ground next to his bed, a cloth full of blood caught his eye. This was something his grandmother had intended to keep secret for the time being, but Vidion now knew. He saw it as the perfect opportunity to scare and convince Laik to help him.

At the same moment, Laik was with his four best friends, and they were trying to build their first raft out of a few pieces of wood they had collected. Together, the five of them loved to seek adventure and were always getting themselves into situations that were dangerous, risky, yet humorous to them. Getting into trouble never mattered to Odum, Gamet and Ian because they did not have parents to punish them. They slept wherever they felt was right for the night, but staying at Elona's home was done more often than not.

Pike, on the other hand, lived with his mother and abusive father. He was the type of person who was not easily embarrassed and often said whatever was on his mind. Most of it was gibberish, but it was frustrating at times. He would often joke during times that jokes were perhaps not the best idea. It was still, however, a quality they loved about Pike, because it usually brought humor to the group, and the boys loved to laugh. Pike was well trained with his hatchet and bow and arrows.

Odum was the tallest of the five. He towered over the rest of them in height and was always the one coming to the rescue. After all, he was so tall that he was often mistaken for an adult. The odd thing about Odum was that he had a rare speech impairment, which only allowed him to say a few specific words. His favorite and most used word was the number seven. For some reason, seven was the answer to most questions he was asked. Chicken was also a favorite word of his, but that came as no surprise because he was indeed obsessed about eating chicken.

Ian, on the other hand, was a drama queen and a victim in his mind, but he was kind and caring. He often said and thought the most ridiculous things, but once again, they accepted each other despite their flaws. Most of Ian's conversations were about his worries, but he also found time to make sure his friends were okay. He was terrible with his hands and building things, but he was decent with a sword.

Then there was Gamet. Gamet was surely the heaviest of the five. He was, admittedly, slightly plump, but he was by far the strongest, bravest, and toughest. Ironically, he hated fat people. He always felt that fat people were friendly only because they were thick and unattractive to most of the villagers. In his mind, it was the only way they could thrive or get what they wanted;

being overly friendly. For that reason, he was often very blunt and straightforward with his conversations and remarks and was very harsh to fat people. He was the only one of the five boys strong enough to wield his half ax and half hammer, which he called Basher.

"Hand me that large, round log over there, would you, Ian?" asked Gamet, who was just about done with the raft.

Ian was confused because, to him, the logs all looked the same. He was terrible with measurements, especially if it meant guessing by eye. "This one?" he tried to confirm, as he pointed at perhaps the smallest log in the pile.

"No, Ian. The one that looks most like your mother." The boys laughed, including Ian. They loved to make fun of one another, and that was probably what made them as close as brothers, to begin with.

Ian was quick with comebacks, and retorted. "Well, maybe if your tits didn't weigh as much as hers, you would be able to get up and get it yourself!"

The boys chuckled, but at that same moment, a rainstorm made its way to their location. They quickly left their unfinished raft and ran for shelter in a cave that was not far from where they were. Pike started a fire to warm them while the rest of them gathered around. "We will have the raft ready in no time, boys. We are almost done," said Laik.

"Yes. So long as Odum stops fantasizing about chicken and Ian learns what the difference between a log and a twig is." Pike was exaggerating, obviously. Ian walked up toward Pike as if he were actually upset and playfully responded.

"I think there is more of a chance that you learn how to bathe before I learn the difference, Pike. As a matter of fact, why don't you stand out in the storm? You might smell better by the time it's over." The boys laughed once again. Pike was known to be a bit on the dirty side. He always seemed to have dirt stains on his clothes and his face as if the villagers used him as a rag. But the boys knew the truth. He usually looked disheveled because of his father, Sid. Sid was a drunk and abusive man, and whenever he was home, Pike found a way to get out. His father would always mistreat him and his mother and even went as far as taking Pike's bed away from him.

For this reason, Pike would mostly sleep on the dirt floor. Most kids his age would have mentally fallen apart, but instead, Pike grew a crude sense of humor. It was how he'd learned to deal with his struggles.

A few hours had passed, and the storm was still running strong. Most of them had fallen asleep, including Laik, whose mind was finally at ease for the first time in a while. Pike lay awake thinking of the raft and all of the fun they would have once it was complete. Still, the thought of adventure was suddenly disrupted when the loud sound of chewing caught his attention. It was Gamet. Pike watched as Gamet tried to sneak a snack into his mouth, not realizing that Pike was awake and watching.

"You got some jelly on your chest, Gamet," he advised, as if he wanted Gamet to know he was awake and watching. Gamet looked down at his shirt and sighed, uttering the words, "Ah crud!" It was a mistake Gamet often made.

The rain stopped, it was dark, and their bellies were rumbling, except for Gamet, who had managed to eat all of their snacks. The boys headed home, vowing to return the following morning to finish the raft. Laik entered his cabin, which was oddly calm and quiet. As he called for his grandmother, Elona's voice arose from her room. Otto was finally sitting up and appeared to be feeling better. Otto smiled at the sight of Laik and spoke to him for the first time in days.

"My boy. How have you been? I trust that you have been behaving yourself." Laik climbed up on the bed next to him in excitement and told him all about the last few days. He was happy to see that his grandfather was doing better and, for a brief moment, forgot about Vidion and his proposal on the ashes. But as the conversation continued, the cloud that had been hovering over Laik returned. In the middle of one of Otto's sentences, he began to cough violently. Laik patted his back like Otto would do for him whenever he coughed. As his grandfather regained his composure and pulled his handkerchief away from his mouth, a bright red stain became the focus in Laik's mind. He pretended not to worry, knowing full well that it was a sign of his grandfather's inevitable death. Otto smiled and lied, assuring him that it was nothing to worry about.

The three of them had gone to bed soon after eating, but Laik couldn't fall asleep after witnessing his grandfather cough blood. A few hours later, his brother Vidion came stumbling in after a few drinks at the local tavern. Laik sat up and faced his older brother with his eyes watered.

"I have decided to help, Vidion... He's coughing blood. Our grandfather is coughing blood... We need to help him." Vidion was elated, but instead pretended to be concerned.

"I agree, brother. I will pack a few things that we will need. It's going to take us a few days to get there, so we are going to have to think of a reasonable excuse. We will leave in two days. Leave the excuse to me."

Laik nodded, but at that very moment, he heard a struggle come from outside. Laik looked out the window and, through the rain, noticed a boy on the ground and another figure standing over him. The boy appeared to be backing away while the other came at him with a leather belt. It was Pike and, without a second thought, Laik rushed toward the door.

4

The Raft

"Get back in, woman! Don't make me tell you again! This boy is a brat and needs to be taught to respect me. He needs to be taught never to disobey me again!" yelled Sid about his son Pike. He yelled at Pike's mother, who was a shy and timid young woman. She had self-esteem lower than the deepest parts of the ocean, and it was all because of Sid. It was the very reason why Pike was in trouble. His father tended to drink to the point of rage, and he would often take it out on his wife. He would belittle her and call her names, and on this night, Sid decided to verbally abuse her to the point where she lowered her head. If she had been a dog, her tail would have been tucked in between her legs as well. Pike stood up to his father for the first time in his life. Pike knew if he did not, his mother would end up with bruises just as bad as Elona's. He had seen it before and knew that he was the only one who could stop it. As Sid reached back to strike his wife, Pike grabbed his arm and accidentally elbowed his father in the face during the struggle. Sid was outraged, and his immediate instinct was to slap his son across the face, knocking him to the ground.

Pike's mother watched in horror, as the person she had once thought was the love of her life began to pummel her only son. As any mother would do, she grabbed a staff and struck her husband over his head, leaving a small gash that drenched his face with his blood. Sid stood up in a daze, and after registering what happened, he charged at her, knocking her over a small table and on to the ground, quivering in pain. By now, Pike was on his feet, ready to use the hatchets that he had trained to use since he was five years old. Sid looked him in the eye and noticed the fear. He knew that his son would not strike him. Sid laughed at the sight of his son trembling, and walked toward him. He placed his palm over his son's face and pushed him hard enough to send him rolling onto the ground. This enraged Pike, but before he could get back up, his father kicked him toward the ground, taking off his belt.

"You have always been a disappointment to me, Pike. Always. You are always in trouble, always defy me, and you have done nothing with the twelve years of your existence. Now you sit here on the ground in pain and unable to protect your mother. A boy like you has no place in this world, but I am stuck with you until one of us dies. Let it be known, you bastard. When I..." His words were interrupted by Laik, who was now running toward him with a sword in his hands.

"Leave him! Leave him or I will slice your throat!" shouted Laik. Sid stopped and looked to see where the voice came from. He chuckled at the sight of him and spit toward the ground before warning Laik not to come any closer. Laik ignored his words and continued to stand up for his friend, who was wounded but determined. In reality, Pike was a much better fighter than Laik and could probably even stop his father as well. The issue with Pike was that, even though he loved to joke about everything, he did not want to strike his father. At the end of the day, Sid was still his father, and his mother had taught him to respect him, no matter what.

Laik stood his ground and unsheathed his sword. With ease, Sid pushed him onto the ground next to Pike, and at this point, Sid lost control of his drunken rage. He charged toward them with a dagger in his hand, but before he could inflict a wound on any of them, Laik swung his blade toward his face. The blade sliced him open over his left eye, leaving him with a cut. Sid regained his balance and charged at them again, but this time, Pike had had enough. For the first time, he struck his father, grabbing his hatchets from his belt and straps and hitting him in the groin with the handle. Sid fell to his knees in pain and realized the ale had gotten to him. He looked at the both of them and grumbled, "I will be back for the both of you, you little punks," as he staggered away into the forest.

Both of them lay flat on the muddy, wet surface and relished every drop of rain that landed on their faces. They looked up at the cloudy skies with their hearts still racing from what had just happened. After a few moments, Laik broke the silence.

"I was in my room speaking to my brother when I heard the ruckus. I'm sorry that this happened to you, Pike, and I'm sorry for using my sword on your father. I just... I just couldn't stand there and watch him do that to you." Pike smiled and thanked his friend.

"I would've done the same thing. He has been hitting my mother more frequently and speaking to me as if I were cow dung. I can't take it anymore, Laik, and the next time I see him, he will not be allowed near my mother."

The boys helped each other up and checked up on Pike's mother. She was still sitting on the floor in tears, shocked at what had just happened. After soothing tea and discussion, she finally fell asleep, and Laik began to head home. Before he left, Laik thought about telling Pike about the old man from the market. He figured it would be best if at least one person knew of his whereabouts just in case something happened to them. After all, they were dealing with an evil sorcerer that was rumored to lurk around a haunted forest. What if it were true?

"Pike... I need to tell you something, but please keep it between us. I'm not supposed to tell anyone, but I could use your help if you don't mind." Pike nodded and continued to listen. "Two days from now, I am going to head toward The Grayfalls. My brother and I ran into an old man who knows of a way to cure my grandparents, but to help us, he needs the ashes of the gods. They are supposedly entombed there. I ask you to please watch over my grandparents. Just make sure they are okay from time to time. I am going to tell them that I will be camping with Odum, Gamet, and Ian because we are expecting this journey to take a few days." Pike assured him that he would check in on Elona and Otto from time to time, and they embraced as if they were brothers who had not seen each other for years.

Laik returned home, and the following morning, his uncle Flint was there attending Otto before Laik even opened his eyes. Flint had agreed to take care of Otto while Elona handled some of the responsibilities and errands of the village. Flint's wife took it upon herself to stay as well and take care of Iolas, whose teeth were beginning to sprout.

"Where are you headed, my boy?" asked Uncle Flint. Laik became nervous and stumbled with his words, but after a few moments, he gathered himself.

"Just some fun with the boys, Uncle. We are going to sleep in the wilderness and practice some of our skills with our bows and arrows."

Laik tossed a few items to eat into his bag and quickly headed toward the river. He and his friends had decided to finish the raft and finally test it out on the water for the first time. While Odum and Ian awaited the rest of them at the stream, Gamet sat impatiently on a chair in front of Pike. Pike was known to sleep until late in the afternoon, and Gamet was left with the task of ensuring that he got up on time. In reality, though, Gamet only wanted to ensure he woke up early enough for them to get some food. Breakfast was his favorite.

Pike's mother tried to rest in another room, exhausted, especially since the night before was very rough and full of conflict. She had spent most of the night tossing and turning until her eyes could not take it anymore, and fell asleep. Pike, on the other hand, was like a log on a stack of hay. He always slept well, but this time Gamet sat there watching and thinking about how he should wake him. The chair underneath him creaked with every subtle movement he made, oblivious to the fact that the chair was not holding his weight very well. Before he knew it, the chair gave way to his weight and crumbled; the sound of it instantly startling Pike. Pike looked at his friend on the ground, the remnants of his favorite chair spread across his room and underneath Gamet's buttocks.

"Thank you, Gamet. Thank you for the lovely start to my day. I would have much preferred you ate my breakfast than break my favorite chair, but thank you. Fat ass," Pike said sarcastically.

Gamet snickered and replied, "Listen, I suspect this chair was simply old, and it was its time to go. More importantly, can we please go get some food? I am starving! I know the guys are waiting for us, and if we brought back some food, they would surely forgive and forget our lateness. Please... Please!" Pike was still dumbfounded at the fact that his chair was shattered.

It was nearly midday before Pike was able to find a bit of money from his father's drawer and meet with the boys at the river. The five of them were starving, but they each cared enough for one another to wait patiently to eat, even though they always found it necessary to bicker.

"It's about damn time!" stated Ian, starting to rant. "Hey, Gamet, did you manage to wake Pike up on time, or did you take long because you decided to eat for five before coming?"

Gamet naturally ignored the fat joke since it was all they ever had on him and replied, "I'll have you know that I woke up on time. It was Pike who decided to sleep in, and once he woke up, he went out of his way to gather a few coins for us to eat. You know very well the market isn't very far from here, so we figured we would put our money together and treat ourselves to a great feast. So... eat my balls, you bastard."

The boys suddenly became excited. The market had the best of foods and treats to eat, and it was not always that they were able to get their hands on money to buy from there. Gamet and Pike tossed their coins on the ground to see how much they had collected. Odum and Laik tossed in a few coins of their own, while Ian desperately searched through his pockets only to reveal a few pieces of lint and crushed rocks. It was usually the case with Ian, and before he was able to announce that he had nothing, Laik started to count. They found that they only had enough to feed two out of the five of them.

Gamet paced back and forth with a look of great concern while the others tried to think of a solution. There was no way a boy as large as Gamet would be able to continue with the raft without a full belly. Ian naturally felt the most pressure among the five of them since he did not make a contribution. Still, before long, Ian devised a plan to make up for it.

The boys arrived at the market, and carefully looked for a vendor who appeared to be sweet and soft-spoken. To their luck, an elderly woman happened to be selling their favorite pastries, which was perfect for the scheme they had planned. Ian grabbed all of the money they had and ordered their food.

"What a great day! Would you please prepare half a roasted chicken for me? You always have the best foods this town has to offer! You are truly gifted at what you do." The old lady smiled and thanked him. She explained that cooking was her passion, and it was something she had loved to do with her mother when she was a little girl. She happily prepared the chicken as Ian continued to order the richest pastries the market had to offer. He ordered a few cakes and fruits for each of them and was even able to afford a few slices of cheese. It was exactly enough for half of the boys, and Ian happily gave her the money. The old woman was pleased with the compliments from Ian and even decided to throw in a few extra goodies at no charge. As she handed him the bag filled with the items of Ian's order, a thief suddenly whooshed in between them and snatched the bag out of her hands. Ian tried to catch him but tripped and found his face submerged into the damp, muddy ground.

It was, of course, all part of the plan. The thief was Pike, but the old woman did not know that. The old lady looked over at Ian, whose tears trickled down his face.

"How am I ever going to feed my family today? My mother... she is sick, and this was all the money we had for the week. How will I feed my baby sister? She is just a baby." The old woman helped him up to his feet and expressed her displeasure and disbelief. Out of kindness, she prepared an extra order of precisely what he had asked for and gave it to him. Ian smiled and wiped the fake tears from his face, taking the food as if he were not part of the selfish and heartless act. He thanked her a thousand times, and off he went to meet with the boys at the raft. By the time Ian arrived, the others were done setting up and were awaiting his arrival. They now had double the amount of food for half the price, and they ate without shame. They enjoyed every minute of it and reminisced about the good old days, which, unbeknownst to them, were about to end. At this point, their raft was complete and ready to test in the water, but it was decided that they would try it out after they rested. Their bellies were filled, and Gamet already seemed to be enjoying an afternoon nap. Ian was next to fall asleep, and before they knew it, they all did.

It was just before dusk when Odum began mumbling the words "Chicken, Chicken, Chicken, Pork, Pork, Pork, Beef, Beef, Beef," over and over again in his sleep. Laik woke to find all of his friends still sleeping. He woke them all, and they were upset because they had slept and wasted the day away. They had worked hard on the raft for days upon days, and each of them had often sacrificed quite a bit of time to get as far as they had with it. At the moment, it was their most valued possession, and although the older folks did not know of their intent, it had always been for the benefit of Toewood. Their raft was built rather large, and they did this to catch as many fish as they could carry. They planned to help ease the burden of hunting and traveling to the bazaar while exploring and having fun with one another. Naturally, the boys also planned to have many

52

adventures and searching for The Bloodstone was at the top of Laik's list.

Laik stretched his arms as high into the air as he could to shake off the sleepiness that was telling him to close his eyes once more. Pike was snoring loudly with his mouth fully open, which Laik saw as an opportunity. He gathered a few small pebbles that were scattered near him and attempted to throw them into Pike's mouth as he quietly snickered to himself. Suddenly, from the corner of his eye, he spotted two figures approaching their raft and speaking softly to one another. Laik dropped the pebbles and quietly snuck up on them to make sure they did not damage or steal the raft they had worked so hard on to finish. He crouched silently behind a nearby shrub and listened as he realized the two men were knights of King Nevil.

"I can't wait to get back to the castle. It's been too long without a proper night's rest and a decent meal. I'm tired of eating berries and rabbits," said one of the knights. The other agreed and spotted the raft lying on the ground without anyone in sight. They decided to chop it up for firewood and set camp for the night. They were only a few hours away from the castle, but with the sun about to set, they figured it would be best to catch some rest. Laik still sat in silence and listened, ready to stop the men if they did begin to destroy their raft. The knights continued to speak.

"If there is anything that I have learned... going forward, I will not listen to anything any villager has to say. I don't care if they are gushing blood and claim an evil monster is at our doorstep. Until I see it, the king will not be disturbed. We are lucky to still have our heads and our positions as knights." The second knight agreed as the first one continued to express his frustration. "It was all that old hag's fault. We listened to her.

I don't know why we listened. I don't know why we allowed her to see the king without receiving a notice. If it weren't for her, we wouldn't have to be going from village to village, collecting additional inconvenience fees and beating the sense into the villagers who oppose the king's word. What was that hag's name again?" he asked his companion.

"I believe it was Elona, but she got what she deserved. I bet it felt great when you beat her half to death and left her in a pool of blood." The knights laughed at Elona's misfortune as their words came together for Laik. They were the men who had left Elona bruised and battered in the cold. Laik's blood began to boil and he jumped out of the bushes without ever thinking about asking his friends for help.

Laik drew his sword on the two men, who were not afraid, but confused at the fact that a child was holding a sword at them. Laik all but foamed at the mouth and practically growled at them. "You are the bastards who beat an old woman! You are the bastards that left my grandmother for dead! I prayed that I would bump into you one day, but I would have never imagined it would happen so soon. I will kill you if it's the last thing I do!" yelled Laik, right before he charged at them with his blade. The two knights were caught off guard, tripped over the raft, and fell into the mud behind it. They quickly tried to get back up to their feet, but even though Laik was just a boy, he acted swiftly with all of his might and knocked them back down. Had it not been for their armor, his sword would have pierced through them several times.

The men crawled backward to create space between them and Laik as they blew their horns to call on the rest of the knights, who were only a few paces away. Within seconds, the rest of them showed up and helped the two up onto their feet again.

All of their weapons were now drawn at Laik, who showed no panic and no distress.

"This little lad made you sound the alarm?" said one of the guards, and laughed at his colleagues' misfortune. The troops walked toward the boy to seize him, but just before they were able to lay their hands on Laik, Odum, Ian, Gamet, and Pike all jumped from the bushes and attacked the knights. The boys were able to hold them off for a good while, but before they knew it, they found themselves with the need to escape. Odum quickly tossed the raft into the water and hurled Laik on. The float was taken by the current of the river, which made it difficult to jump on. Still, one by one, the boys leaped onto the raft. Last to jump on board was Gamet, who somehow made the time to grab the last of the food they put away for later. As the boys sailed off, the knights threw stones and shouted at them. The boys laughed, and then laughed even harder as Pike taunted the knights by showing them his buttocks.

That night, as the river continued to take them all down-stream, they had strengthened their bond even though they didn't know it. The boys had risked their lives for one another and laughed as they recalled the looks on the faces of the guards. They celebrated the fact that their raft worked and had come in handy in the nick of time. Laik turned to Odum and thanked him for tossing him onto the raft. Had it not been for Odum, he probably would have stayed trying to kill the knights who had hurt Elona. Laik would have likely taken a spear to his stomach. After some time, the boys decided to stop along the edge of the river. They felt they had traveled a safe distance from the knights and hid the raft behind a few shrubs for them to retrieve another day. The five of them kept a watchful eye as they trekked back home, and they shared stories of past times and memories that they treasured with each other, like the time they'd all tried as a group to lift Odum. He was so large that it was the only way they stood a chance at picking him up. In the process, Odum released a large amount of hot gas from his backside. Ian happened to be at the receiving end and swallowed it whole on his next breath. The boys dropped Odum because they were laughing so hard at Ian's misfortune, while Ian spent the next few hours gagging and spitting every few seconds.

When they finally reached home, Toewood was dead silent, and all of the villagers were sound asleep. The boys tried their best not to wake anyone as they approached Pike's home first. Odum noticed the front door to Pike's home was busted open while the boys said their last few jokes and insults to each other. "Odum," he bellowed, pointing toward the open door. The boys looked over to see what Odum was pointing at, and Pike's heart sank at the sight of his home. "Mom... Mom?" cried Pike as he ran toward his house. A sudden eerie feeling took over the rest of them as they followed their friend inside. There, they found his mother beaten and battered. Worse, the same dagger Sid had tried to use on Pike was found on the ground next to her and her stomach was bleeding profusely.

"Who did this, Mother? What happened?!" asked Pike as he begged for answers. His mother was barely able to speak but managed to find the strength to tell her son that it was Sid. Once again drunk, Sid had returned as promised to get his revenge on Pike and Laik, but they were not there. Instead, he found his wife, who was alone and defenseless. Pike expressed his love and gratitude to his mother, knowing that her last breaths were upon her, and when she died in his arms, his friends were there to comfort him as best as they could. Pike now had no family and nowhere to go. He searched the entire night for his father, but it was as if he was now a ghost. He was nowhere to be found.

Pike did not say a word the entire night, and the boys stayed with him on the front porch. They knew burying his own mother would be difficult for him, so Odum and Gamet took it upon themselves to bury her body behind their home. Not a single villager was aware of the events, and as the morning sun rose above the hills, the boys remained the only ones who knew. The five of them were still sitting on the porch when the bright sun reminded Laik of the journey to come.

"Pike... I know that you likely do not want to do or say anything, but you shouldn't stay here. You shouldn't stay alone. I'm going to ask my brother if you could come with us. Maybe it will help keep your mind busy," said Laik. Pike nodded yes hesitantly, and the rest of the boys stayed with Pike while Laik headed home.

Vidion was outside waiting for him to leave on their journey, both of their bags ready at his feet. It was as if he did not want his younger brother to go inside, which, Laik supposed, made sense. Why risk waking his grandparents up? Why risk getting caught and grounded? Regardless, Laik asked his older brother if he could quietly and carefully enter his home for a few minor necessities, but Vidion opposed the idea. He insisted they had to go at once, but before they did, Laik explained what had happened to Pike. Vidion did not care in the slightest.

"Listen, Laik. We can't afford to take more people. The more of us that disappear, the more they will notice. You need to think about Grandma. You need to think about Grandpa. Pilk will be fine," said Vidion.

"His name is Pike; not Pilk," replied Laik.

"Same thing! The point is... think about your family, Laik. There is nothing you can do for your friend. His mother is dead... he will be here with your other friends, and he will be fine. Your family, however, needs you. You can be the one to bring back their health and give them what they need to live forever." Laik's mind became filled with the thought of death once more, and he obeyed his older brother. It was against his better judgment, but he advised the other boys that he had to leave. Pike, of course, knew where he was headed to, but remained silent as the others stayed to comfort him. He understood, but before Laik left, Pike spit out the last ounce of hope he had for seeing his mother alive. "If it's possible, Laik... and this journey of yours proves to be real, see if there is something to bring back my mother... she was all I had." Laik embraced his friend, and before long, he and his brother Vidion were off to Grayfalls Forest.

5

Grayfalls

The sun had finally climbed over the hills as Laik dragged his feet behind Vidion. His eyes were heavy from the restless night. The brothers walked in silence toward Grayfalls forest as Vidion thought about the things to come and the things he was about to do to get them. Laik, on the other hand, remained with the thought of death and wondered where Pike's mother was at that moment. Was she in the heavens with the gods, or had she simply ceased to exist? While he thought, Vidion looked for the words to break the silence. He needed to plant his seed, but was not sure how to convince Laik. He knew that he was only helping him to cure their grandparents, and that was what was most important to him.

"Don't worry, Laik. I know you're tired and worried, but soon we will have the ashes and a cure for Otto. Once we have the cure, he and Elona won't have to suffer anymore, and we can move on with our lives. Nothing is going to stop our grandparents, and the village will be back to normal." Laik smiled at the thought and agreed, which was precisely what Vidion wanted. Vidion paused and pretended to be concerned.

He purposefully sighed loudly and looked toward the ground as if he were troubled, hoping for Laik to ask him what was wrong. Of course, it worked, especially since they were on the topic of their grandparents.

"What's wrong, Vidion? Are you not happy at the fact that we have a chance to cure them?" This was the perfect opening for Vidion, and he took the opportunity with arms wide open.

"I sure am, my brother... but I couldn't help but think... could you imagine if we had a way to make them both live forever?" Laik's interest was immediately piqued as the thought of having his grandparents around forever made him smile with glee.

"Of course," said Laik.

"Well, I was thinking. What if there was a way? What if we could make that happen? All we would have to do is keep some of the ashes without anyone knowing. Ghaldon could then help me become a sorcerer, and I could use that power to heal. I could use that power and become even stronger than Ghaldon himself. I would make our grandparents live forever, and you would never have to worry."

The sound of this enticed Laik. It was the one thing that was always on his mind these days; death, and for the first time, a solution was presented. But the idea of eternal life for all of his loved ones soon came to a halt as he recalled the story Elona once told him. Ghaldon was a deceiver. He was selfish, and was cursed and trapped within the haunted forest because of his greed. The last thing Laik wanted was to see Vidion in a similar set of shoes.

"We can't do it, Vidion. We can't trust Ghaldon to help us in that way, and we don't know how the ashes would affect you. What if it killed you or put a curse on your soul just like it did to him? Our grandparents would die without a cure, and you would be lost forever. I would be alone, and I would never be able to forgive myself."

Vidion's blood began to boil. He knew Laik was right, but the way he saw it was that they were only possibilities. It was also possible for him to get what he wanted, and he was mentally prepared to do what was necessary to get it. He calmly tried to regain a soft and caring tone and responded.

"Yes. That is true. But sometimes things need to be done for the greater good. Look at our grandmother, for instance. She risked her life just to gain easier access to the market and almost lost her life for it. I would, of course, have hated that, but she risked it all for us. She is a hero, Laik. We could be that and so much more. No one would ever have to suffer, and I think I know how to do this and get out in one piece." Laik looked at his brother and waited for his plan. "We kill Ghaldon. After he concocts the potion, we simply drink it ourselves!"

"No... No, Vidion. He is a powerful sorcerer, and he would kill you and me within the blink of an eye. We need to save our grandparents; not become heroes." Vidion snapped and quickly yelled back at his younger brother.

"It's not like he can tell the future! He won't know what we have planned!" Laik looked at him with a face of disappointment. It was the first time he had looked at his brother with displeasure, and the look on his face told Vidion that he was losing the discussion. He knew he needed Laik more than Laik could imagine, and that this was a task that he could not do alone. Vidion pretended to be embarrassed by his actions. Still, he managed to convince Laik that it was all out of fear and worry for their grandparents. Although it was upsetting for him to see, Laik forgave his older brother and put the argument behind them. The boys stood at the edge of Grayfalls forest as Vidion followed the scroll to where the ashes were rumored to be. Despite the fear and anxiety in Laik's eyes, his heart stayed strong with the love and courage he possessed to help his grandfather. But what he did not know was that it was already too late.

Otto lay lifeless on his bed, which Vidion had discovered before they left. That had been the real reason Vidion had refused to let his brother in the house and urged him to head toward the Grayfalls forest immediately. Vidion knew that Laik would not have left if he had seen his grandfather's lifeless body, and the hoped-for days of him being a powerful sorcerer would never come. Elona awoke shortly after the boys went and grabbed a cup of hot tea. Iolas was under the care of Uncle Flint for the night, so it was the first cup of tea she was able to enjoy in a while. Above the tealeaves, Vidion had left a note, which excused their absence. He lied and wrote that Laik and he had gone to catch some fish on the new raft. Once she had finished reading the note, Elona asked Otto several times if he would like some tea, but there was no response. It was odd for him not to respond because he was usually the first to wake up, and it was not like Otto to leave unannounced. Otto was also sick and bedridden. Elona checked on her husband and found him asleep, but just before she turned and walked away, she noticed a small trail of dirt, in the form of shoeprints. Elona followed the dirt back to the boys' room, where the path suddenly stopped. After looking around the room, she found a print on top of a small nightstand that Vidion used. She became curious and looked up to notice the edge of a small chest peeking over a beam of wood. Elona carefully climbed on top of the nightstand and grasped it. Inside she found four small bottles, and they were labeled as mercury. It was enough mercury to poison someone ten times over, but the more she thought, the more she wondered why Vidion had such a thing and in such a large amount. Then it hit her.

Since the death of Myla and Quinn, Vidion had offered to help around the house, which was odd for him. He hesitantly took on several chores that she asked of him. Still, the one thing he took a particular interest in was serving the food. Elona sat at the edge of his bed, praying that it was not so. But she began to think that Vidion had slowly poisoned his very own grandfather. She carefully tried to place the box back in its place of origin, but as she took a step off of the nightstand, her bracelet became tangled with the chest and down it went. The chest cracked, and the bottles shattered into pieces. As Elona watched the remaining ounces of mercury seep into the wood floor, she noticed a letter hidden where the chest was now cracked. It was a note written by Vidion, and on it was a list of dosages and the amount of time it would take to kill a person. At the bottom, Vidion scribbled the name of his grandfather, and each day he added the mercury to his food. Elona sat in silence and frustration as she crumpled the note and squeezed it with all of her might. The reality of her husband's death finally hit her, and what made it worse was that he had never really been sick. It had been a murder, by the hands of her very own grandson.

At the front gates of Toewood, a villager neared the end of his night watch as he tried desperately to stay awake. The cool, comfortable temperature did not help, of course, and the night was quiet and calm. At a distance, a few torches began to light the path toward Toewood. The guard figured it was likely a few villagers returning home for the night and dozed off into a slumber. He could not stay awake any longer. Within a few minutes, the number of torches began to increase by the dozen,

63

and not a soul in Toewood was aware of them. Elona still sat at the edge of Vidion's bed as she began to hear and feel the steps of those who approached. The fires from the torches were now in the view of the bedroom window, and as she peeked over the sill, she found that the men who were upon them were knights of King Nevil. The army stopped in the middle of the village; some of the people now awake. Their leader dismounted from his horse and looked through a window as if he were looking for someone in particular. After a few moments, Elona recognized the man in charge. It was the knight that beat her and the same man that was embarrassed by Laik and his friends. "I come here in the name of the king. We are seeking the old woman by the name of Elona, her grandchildren, and all of her family. Show yourself, and you may live to see another day. Hide, and you surely will not."

Elona closed her eyes to help her think. She knew nothing about what Laik had done but knew that the demand for her and her family at such an odd hour was not a good sign. She was sure they would kill her if not now, then at the feet of the king. After a while, the knights grew tired of waiting; their torches were still burning bright. As the general made a hand signal, a few of their horses pulled in a wagon, and out the men pulled the thickest of tree trunks and oil. The knights quickly barricaded every cabin and cottage in Toewood and doused them with oil, as the cries of the villagers inside them began to grow louder and louder. Toewood was set ablaze without a second warning, and almost the entire population was burned alive. The knights stayed to make sure of it and watched as the town collapsed. Some of the people managed to escape through their windows, but the archers executed them as they crawled out. As if that were not cruel enough, the knights were ordered to dig out and collect the bones from all of the graves in Toewood. This included the remains of Quinn and Myla.

The two brothers reached the entrance to the cave where the ashes of the gods were rumored to be. Vidion lit a torch for each of them and led the way into the darkness. The cave was cold and wet, and drops of water plopped onto their heads as if an ocean seeped above them through the rock. It was undoubtedly as old as the stories said, because the stalagmites and stalactites were enormous. Most of them formed pillars and columns that resembled all sorts of things to those with an imagination. To Laik, it was rare and beautiful, but Vidion paid no mind as he crushed and smashed the calcium-based formations to get what mattered to him most. After a few hours of wandering through the dark cave, the brothers reached what appeared to be a dead end. Vidion grew frustrated as he further studied the map for any turns or twists he might have missed. A warm yet strong gust of air whooshed its way through the canals of the cave, and out their torches went. Usually, Laik was not afraid of the dark, but the blackness of an unlit cave was something that he had never experienced before. While he scrambled to relight his torch, Vidion's voice could be heard cursing and bickering at the misfortune. Then, out of the darkness, a deep and monstrous growl echoed through the cave. Laik froze and looked around the dark room, hoping for a show of light. Instead, the warm breeze brushed against his skin again, which was strange because they were in a cold cave in the middle of winter.

"What was that? The growl; was it a monster?" asked Laik as if Vidion knew.

"How the hell should I know? ... Don't cower on me, Laik. It was probably just the wind howling. Our torches just blew out

65

because of it." The brothers reignited their torches, and Vidion continued to look at the map. At the same time, Laik carefully walked toward the direction of the warm breeze. He was scared, but he certainly did not want his brother to know it.

At the dead end, he noticed a ledge above him that was just within his reach. It was practically hidden because of the cave formations. Laik pulled himself up, scuttled through a crawlspace, and at the end of it dropped down into a gulley. It appeared as if the trail continued, and the path was well lit with a fire that glowed an odd blue-gray color. The area was warm, which explained where the breeze came from. Laik figured the warmth came from the flames and trekked back the way he came; his brother was still fuming at the map.

"Vidion! Vidion! I found it! The rest of the way is here!" hollered Laik. Vidion rushed over and followed his brother into the ditch.

Once again, the growl could be heard, but this time even closer than before. Vidion continued to be adamant about it being the wind as the boys finally reached the spot on the map that Vidion was looking for. His eyes opened wide and glistened as he tried desperately to hide his excitement and thirst for power.

"This is it, Laik. This is it! This is where your part in this journey comes into play," he said, pointing at a crevice that led into another room. "This is the tomb of the gods. The ashes of Wyolus, Flonius, Erthos, and Airos rest just beyond it. All you have to do now is take these four bottles, find their ashes and bring as much as you can back to me... Here... take an extra bottle just in case."

Laik swallowed what felt like the core of an apple as he grabbed the bottles and squeezed himself through the crack. His brother ensured that he would be there waiting as he passed over one of the torches to Laik. Inside, the warm air once again filled the room, and with the dim light of his torch, he found a ring of torches and set them afire so that the entire room lit up. In the center, yet another opening led him to a maze of caverns, which took him more time to travel through than either of them had thought. Vidion waited impatiently outside for his brother's return, pacing back and forth like a mad man. Vidion practically salivated at the thought of power and the things he wanted to do.

After what felt like an eternity, Laik unearthed the doors to the tomb. They were old and rusty, and they resembled those of a cellar or basement. After all, it was a crypt, and it was built ages ago. The doors creaked open, and down the stone steps he went. At the very end, four altars sat elevated against the back wall, and on top of them sat a statue of the corresponding god. Each statue held an urn, and within these, the ashes rested, untouched by man for centuries.

The ground was coated with a thin layer of water that was no deeper than the nail on his thumb, and every step he took made the sound 'plit, plat, plit, plat'. Laik walked up the five steps and carefully opened the urns, looking over his shoulder because of the strange eerie feeling that something was watching him. Laik cautiously opened the pouch his brother had given him and began to fill the bottles with the sacred ashes. As he slipped the final one back into his pouch, a sudden fear and overwhelming doubt began to take over his thoughts. He was afraid of his brother. He did not trust him, and the idea of him possessing the ashes started to feel like something he should not allow. He tried to find a possible explanation in his mind, but every excuse he came up with became disproven by another. It was then that it clicked for Laik. The only reason Vidion was here was for

67

himself. He did not care about a cure for their grandparents. Not once had he ever seemed to care for them or their well-being. It was all self-interest and a desire for power. It had to be, as much as he did not want to believe it.

After a few moments of pondering and wondering if his brother would deceive him, Laik took out another bottle and filled it with dirt he found near the altar. It looked almost identical to the ashes of Erthos. With that, he stepped back into the water and started the hike back to Vidion. Once again, all he could hear was the plit and plat of his steps on the water, but near the stone steps that took him back up, the growl could be heard louder than ever.

Laik refused to look behind him and closed his eyes, as if not looking would make whatever made the sound disappear. He continued to walk and came to a sudden stop to see if he would hear it again, but the sound he heard then was even eerier than the growl itself. From right behind him, he could hear the steps, and they stopped only after he did. The hairs on the back of his neck stood up. He was sure there was something behind him, but did not wish to look back to find out. He quickly splashed through the rest of the way and hurried up the steps, slamming the cellar-like doors shut behind him. From down below, the creature growled so loud, the doors began to shake as Laik jammed it shut with a stick that rested on the ground, but it was all for nothing. The creature was the protector of the crypt, created and placed there eons ago by Knilan himself. Its name was Klokus.

Its purpose was to ensure that no man got a hold of the ashes, because man was greedy. After all, Knilan knew that the wicked would attempt to use them for themselves, and the virtuous would be cast aside with such great power.

Klokus burst through the doors like magma from a volcano, knocking Laik flat on his back. It was the first time in his life that he had seen a monster, standing tall with his clay-like skin yet rock-like frame. Klokus was slow but dangerous, and it started to charge toward Laik. Laik quickly jumped to his feet and ran through the maze of caverns, miraculously remembering the way to his brother. The fact that Vidion had lied to him was temporarily out of his mind as he desperately tried to outrun Klokus. The beast was so massive, it smashed and shattered nearly everything that was in its way. It was much easier for Laik to run through the caverns because of his small size, but Klokus was almost four times the size of a man.

Every boulder he crushed put them in danger, as the cave began to collapse within itself. Laik could now see the opening and his brother peeking through the other side, yelling at him to hurry. It seemed as if he would make it, but all of a sudden, Laik was pulled back by the ankle, thrown against the limestone wall, and became trapped in a landslide of dirt and rock. Laik remained silent as he watched Klokus from inside. The beast tried to pick up his scent, but the layers of soil and rock were too thick for it to pinpoint where he was. Not long after, Vidion managed to find a way from the other side of the rubble and quietly announced himself to his brother, who was desperately searching for a way out.

"Psst... psst. Laik. Stay low. Crawl over here. Quiet."

Laik's eyes opened wide with a sigh of relief as he crawled as close as he could to Vidion, who spoke to him through yet another crevice.

"There is no time, Laik. Give me the ashes. Give me the ashes, and I will return with help. If you stay quiet, that monster won't be able to find you. Give the pouch to me, Laik. Toss it to me now!" he demanded.

Then the thoughts of betrayal resurfaced. Every second that Laik held on to the bottles outraged his older brother, who placed more worth on the ashes than his very own brother. After the back and forth, Vidion began to guilt-trip him.

"You must give me the ashes, Laik. If you don't, our grandparents are going to die. You wouldn't want them to die, would you?"

Laik hesitantly agreed and handed the bottles over to Vidion through the crack. He wanted to believe that his thoughts were wrong, but his feelings were soon proven true. An evil grin formed from ear to ear as Vidion stared at his little brother with the look of death in his eyes.

"You will be back, right, brother?" asked Laik.

"Since before the day you were born, I have yearned for the moment when I would be on my own. A day where our mother and Quinn wouldn't force me to do things I didn't want to do, a day when I didn't have to pretend to like you and a day when I no longer had to worry about Elona and Otto," Vidion cynically whispered to his brother. Laik felt betrayed as he continued to listen to what his brother had to say.

"You see, Laik... Otto doesn't need a cure. There is nothing wrong with him. I poisoned him. I've been poisoning him for a while now, and the reason we left in a hurry was because... he is dead. But don't worry, Laik. Elona is as good as dead as well. Do you remember the guards you embarrassed not long ago? I watched the whole thing, and I told them. I told them who you were and where you lived, and even told them about your friends. By now, everyone you love should be dead, and soon you will be, too." Laik looked at him in horror and was barely able to speak.

70

"... Why?" he asked as his world felt as if it were coming to an end. Everyone he knew and loved was presumed dead, and now, he was about to face his biggest fear all by himself; his own death.

"Why? Were you not able to figure that out on your own? I don't like you, Laik. I never did. You were a mistake. You ruined my life the day you were born, and it's crazy to think: I was there the day you came into this life, and now, I am here on the day you will leave. I bid you farewell, brother. I am off to become more powerful than any god that has ever roamed on this planet." Laik held back the tears as he watched his brother step back and blow his horn. Klokus growled at the sound, searching and sniffing in Laik's area. Laik stayed as quiet as quiet could be as he closed his eyes and prayed that none of what Vidion had mentioned was true. Then, he remembered. One of the bottles never made it back into the pouch. The ashes of Erthos remained in his hand, while the placebo rested in Vidion's. Laik leaned against a boulder while Klokus continued to hunt for his scent. He tried his best not to think about his death, and the only thing that seemed to work at the moment was the thought of his friends. He thought to himself that if Vidion was telling the truth, they were now the only people he could trust, and they were the only people he could rely on.

6

The Clearing of the Haze

"Loyalty has nothing to do with blood, idiot!" yelled Pike as he tried to explain that even family members betray one another. Ian was convinced of the opposite. His entire life, he had been taught that family came first no matter what, but for people like Pike, it wasn't right.

"Look at my father, Ian. Do you consider him loyal? The man spent his entire life punching me in the face, and sometimes it was for his enjoyment. I once asked if I could play outside with my friends, and he responded by bashing my head against the wall! I woke up the following morning, bleeding from the nose, with my mother right next to me."

Ian was at a loss for words as he pictured the scenario in his head. It was the first time he had considered the possibility that loyalty had nothing to do with kinship. Gamet listened and laughed as he poked fun at Ian for being so naïve.

"If I didn't know any better, Ian, I would guess that you stopped drinking from your mother's breast only two days ago. You probably still wear a washcloth around your waist to prevent you from soiling yourself," Gamet exclaimed as he chowed down on his favorite pastry.

"And if I didn't know any better, you have likely gained fifteen pounds in the last three minutes, you fat ass." The boys laughed at each other and enjoyed the evening doing so. It was one of the few things that brought them closer; the ability to laugh at one another and not take it personally. After they finished their food, the four of them fixed the slight damage the raft had endured during their encounter with the knights. Death was something they had managed to escape because they left Toewood without anyone knowing.

From a distance, they could see the red and orange blaze, but figured it was just a fire their people had started on their own. From time to time, the villagers would burn parts of a forest to create space for planting or livestock.

Odum still had a mouth full of chicken as Ian broke the temporary silence.

"I know it hasn't been long since we last saw Laik, but I wish he were here. This is a great night." The rest of them agreed.

"He is like our moral compass. I always go to him for advice and reasoning, and he always knows exactly what to say." The boys smiled as Ian continued. Ian noticed the fact that Pike smirked and held back his thoughts.

"What? What do you have to say, Pike? Go on and say it."

"I was just going to say that it borderline sounds like you want to kiss him," Pike said while Odum and Gamet exploded with laughter, "...but I agree with you, Ian. He does try to do the right thing, no matter what. I think you have a great heart, Ian. Even though we make fun of you because of your lack of experience, you are brilliant and kind. You have always been there for each of us during our worst moments. And you know what I like about talking to you, Ian?" Ian sat and listened with glee as his self-confidence was boosted, especially since compliments were seldom a thing amongst this group of friends. "I like that you are not biased. We all know you believe in the gods, but you know that we don't, and you refrain from forcing that on us. You're very clever, even though you don't know how to wipe your ass." The boys once again thundered with laughter at the unexpected insult.

"Pike, the same should apply to you. You are very smart. Very. I've never met someone who can teach himself so many things just by observing. You are great with your hands, and that includes everything from building to fighting. You are like stone, strong and nearly unbreakable," said Gamet as he paused and thought about the things Pike had gone through. "Even though we are all without parents, I don't think I would have been able to handle my mother's death the way you have. I look up to you, Pike." Once again, they agreed and turned their focus on Odum, who was still working on his chicken as he listened.

"Odum, you barely speak, but you have been around longer than any of us have. You are the first in this group, and if it weren't for you, we probably would have never met each other. It's like you're our father... even though you're the same age," said Gamet. Odum continued to listen as he mumbled,

"Odum. Chicken. Seven. Seven. Odum. Chicken."

"Although you barely speak, you are like our protector, and we have all witnessed how you put your life on the line to ensure ours are safe," finished Gamet.

Ian smiled and looked at Gamet.

"...You, Gamet. You know what's great about you?" Gamet sighed and responded,

"Let me guess. I'm fat. Why do I always get the fat jokes

when Odum is fat as well?"

"Because Odum keeps his mouth shut." Pike jokingly intervened.

"I was going to say your honesty, Gamet. You are so honest and blunt that it is refreshing. If we ever want a real opinion, we go to you. If that's not enough to be proud of, you are the strongest of us all! I don't know where you get your strength and sheer brute force from, but it is almost supernatural," said Ian. He continued to mention how Gamet was as cold as ice when it came to affection, but everyone knew Gamet loved his friends like no other. He was like the glue that held their bond together. Whenever there was a quarrel, Gamet was there to hit them with the truth and force them to bury the hatchet. He was always there to help them realize that, in the end, they were all still brothers.

Pike gazed off into the distance as a purple glow grabbed his attention. Gamet noticed the look in Pike's eyes and turned his eyes in the same direction. The purple radiance began to grow as the four boys watched and waited.

It came from the haunted forest, and Vidion was indeed the one responsible for it. After he had retrieved the ashes, he rode to the murky woods as fast as he could to meet with Ghaldon. At the edge of the woods, Vidion hesitated for a brief moment as he thought about the fact that he could find himself stuck within the mist forever, but he was determined. He was determined to obtain the power of the gods, and his greed was more potent than his wits. Vidion opened the bottles of ashes and coated his knife with each of them, hoping that the ashes would kill Ghaldon, should he defy him. The ashes seemed to affect the steel, as they became one with the blade and turned into a dark-colored stone. The bottles were sealed once again, and Vidion hid the knife in his boot.

Within a few moments, Vidion found himself surrounded by the dark lavender flames that the boys saw from a distance. The shadow that lurked in the forest was now in Vidion's sight, and it grew closer and closer. The fire gave way once the shadow approached, and for the first time, Vidion laid his eyes on Ghaldon. Vidion knelt and presented the ashes to him, but he did not kneel of respect or fear. It was to ease his reach to the knife in his boot. Ghaldon snatched the ashes from his hands without acknowledging his presence. The lack of respect left a bad taste in Vidion's mouth because, in his mind, Ghaldon owed him. In his mind, if it were not for him, the ashes would have never touched his fingertips, and Ghaldon needed Vidion more than Vidion needed Ghaldon. Despite his raging anger, Vidion bit his tongue and respectfully began to speak to him. "Great Ghaldon, master of all that lives and breathes in this world, my name is Vidion and—"

"I know who you are, Vidion. You are a bitter boy who is here to collect what was promised. I am not one to stray from my promises. With these ashes, you will become the greatest healer this world has ever seen. They will free me from the walls of this forest, and only you will be spared as long as you vow to serve me." Vidion rose to his feet and walked toward Ghaldon slowly, with his permission. The sorcerer listened to Vidion's words as he began to brew his elixir with the ashes of the gods.

"I traveled a great distance to get these ashes for you. Along the way, I lost my younger brother to the beast known as Klokus. I tried to save him, but I couldn't. It was much too powerful for me. I ask... I beg... that you help me avenge my brother's death by making me more than just a healer, Ghaldon. I wish to become as powerful as you and kill that monster. That beast has taken the last of my family. I now have no one, just like you. After all, if it were not for me, you would not have the ashes at your disposal."

Ghaldon looked at him in disbelief. It was the first time he had been talked down to as a sorcerer. Still, Ghaldon kept his composure, and instead of ending his life with a snap of his fingers, he told Vidion a story about greed.

"Do you how your home Toewood got its name?" asked Ghaldon. Vidion stopped and listened. He did not know how Toewood got its name and figured he would pretend to care and listen in hope that Ghaldon would grant him his request.

"This is a story about greed. It reminds me of you, Vidion, because many years ago, the forefather of your hometown was not satisfied with what he had. He lived alone in these lands, and he had nothing but his hut, a cottage that was worn and torn. His name was Tye, and he was an ambitious young man. The life of poverty was not what he wanted for himself, so he began to sell the one thing he could get plenty of; wood. He sold the lumber at very reasonable prices, and the lumber was a necessity, especially during the winter. He soon realized the need for firewood during the cold months, and gradually raised the cost by triple. Families would freeze to death while he enjoyed the warmth of the fire and started a family of his own. They stayed safe and warm in a new home he built for himself. The people grew angry with him because of the ridiculous cost, but there was nothing they could do. By this time, Tye had nearly complete control of the woods around him, and hired guards to prevent the people from chopping his timber. Then came Zalia, the same goddess that trapped me in this wretched forest. Chopping wood and taking trees down for life's necessities was never an issue with her, but when she learned of Tye's actions and greed for wealth, she gave him the chance to stop. She gave him the chance to fix things, but like most men, Tye was greedy. He refused and continued his control over the firewood. After four days, Zalia returned, and without warning, his tongue was pulled out of his mouth to ensure his words would never poison the thoughts of men. His ability to hear was taken from him, and with it, his sight. Lastly, Zalia cut the toes off his feet so that he could never roam through her woodlands again. His wife eventually left him for another man, and his kids were taken from him too. Tye spent the rest of his days in silence and was left to think about the people he harmed until the day he died. The tale was passed on from village to village, and from this story, the people dubbed your home Toewood."

Vidion stood in confusion and asked,

"And what does this story have to do with me? I don't care about Toewood, and my request has nothing to do with others. It is for me. I want the power! I want revenge!"

"You are asking for more power than was already offered. That is how tyranny begins. You are not satisfied with what you already have. You want more. What you ask of me is to give you my power. You ask that I make you more powerful than I am, and it is something I will not do. You will learn never to ask in greed or selfishness again, for I will no longer grant you the gift of a healer."

Ghaldon finished the potion and placed it on a stone slab. Vidion took a few steps back as Ghaldon walked toward him with an evil grin. Suddenly, Vidion recalled the knife in his boot and kneeled before Ghaldon, who stopped right in front of him.

"I realize what I have done, and I am prepared to accept my punishment, but I beg you, Ghaldon. I beg that you allow me to share my story before you punish me with whatever may come. I doubt it will change your mind, but I pray that, unlike Zalia, you show the compassion that you should have received years ago."

Ghaldon paused for a moment and thought about his words. He hated Zalia and wished to be nothing like her. Vidion knew it, and Ghaldon granted him a few moments to speak.

"Make it quick, Vidion, but I'm warning you. If your story is irrelevant, your punishment will be worse than what you are about to receive."

"Yes, Ghaldon. There is a point to my story. My story is about betrayal. There was this boy I once knew who had everything he ever wanted. He was healthy, and his family loved him, and above all, he was an only child. All gifts and attention were directed toward him, and he loved it. Until one day, his mother announced the arrival of a younger brother. Things changed. The boy took a back seat, and everything was soon shared between the two. As if things could not get any worse, the boy's mother then had a third child, but by this time, the boy had developed a heart as cold as ice. He hated his family, and he hated his brothers for taking away his happiness. Soon after, the boy began to plot. He realized that the only way he would get his happiness back was to be rid of his family."

Odum, Pike, Ian and Gamet had followed the purple blaze to the edge of the forest with their shields and weapons. The four of them debated whether or not the myth and stories were true. The only one who believed in the supernatural was Ian, so they were not very concerned about being trapped in the forest forever. On the other hand, Pike had a strange gut-wrenching feeling that Laik was somehow tied to the strange lights. Pike decided not to let his friends down and entered, the others

79

following behind him. The four of them hid behind the trees as they approached Ghaldon and Vidion—to their utter surprise. They were shocked to see the sorcerer, and for the first time, they began to wonder if all of Elona's stories were true. Both Ghaldon and Vidion were unaware of their presence, and the story continued.

"The boy spent many moons thinking about how he could get rid of his family, and soon came to the conclusion that it would be best to kill them all. On a cold night, his parents traveled to the market for goods that the village needed, but as the time ticked by, the boy's parents never returned. The boy had changed the course of the trail, and his parents became lost in an already unforgiving path. The horses were spooked off the ledge, and the boy watched his parents hold on for dear life. The boy could have saved them, and his parents saw that, but instead, he wished them farewell and pushed the teetering carriage, sending them to their demise. Not long after, the boy poisoned his grandfather and ratted out the whereabouts of his grandmother. King Nevil had been looking for her after his guards were attacked and humiliated by the boy's younger brother. While the guards marched toward her village, the boy took his younger sibling on a quest, and that quest led him here. In case you are not following, Ghaldon, I am the boy. I killed my family, and a great beast is mauling my younger brother to pieces... but this is not necessarily a story of betrayal because of what I have done."

Gamet, Pike, Odum, and Ian looked at each other in disbelief, although they managed to stay quiet and listen to the rest of the story. Ghaldon was so into Vidion's tale that his guard was let down as the tale concluded.

"Though I left my brother at the Grayfalls to die... this is a story of betrayal because... you trusted me with the ashes." Vidion drew his knife and popped up to his feet. His knife pierced through Ghaldon's chest and into his heart. The only way to kill an immortal being was indeed with the power of the gods.

"...and for trusting me, you will die, Ghaldon. I tried to be fair, but you did not give me what I asked for. Now I will have it all for myself as you watch and wither away." Ghaldon collapsed to the ground, watching as the life left his eyes, and Vidion crept toward the chalice filled with the power of the gods. Vidion chugged the potion, making sure that every drop was accounted for and swallowed. The purple blaze grew tenfold as a storm of the same color began to form. The four friends held on for dear life, and the winds, the fire, the rain, and the grounds thundered all around them. Vidion grew in size, and the boys watched his silhouette form into a creature that was twice the size of a man. They kept their eyes on him as he ran off into the darkness, the storm coming to a stop soon after.

The boys found themselves trapped under the remains of rock and trees as they worked together to free one another. "I never liked that bastard! I never did!" yelled Gamet, who was covered from head to toe in dirt. The four of them were enraged as they quickly helped each other out and discussed what to do.

"If his story was true, then King Nevil and his men are likely headed toward Toewood. They will show no mercy to our village. If it were a lie, we would be wasting our time by returning there. They would all be okay. Either way, there is nothing we could do against King Nevil's army. It only makes sense to head to the Grayfalls and look for Laik," suggested Pike. The rest of them agreed unanimously as they watched Ghaldon's body turn into ash before their very eyes. Scared, they rushed toward Laik and away from the body in hope of saving their friend. They were Laik's only hope for survival and, unbeknownst to Vidion, the only ones who knew of his whereabouts.

Laik had grown extremely weak after three days of no food or water. He was exhausted from barely any sleep as well. Klokus had given up the search for Laik, but rested within two arms' reach of him. From time to time, Klokus let out a snarl that was loud enough to hear from the outside of the cave. The sound escaped through an opening at the peak of the mountain that stood over them. The mountain was the smallest one in the area, but still large enough to be considered a mountain and not a hill. The boys followed the snarls up to the peak, knowing that Laik was trapped with some sort of monster.

The crevice where the noise escaped from was well hidden and difficult to find. By the time the boys arrived, Klokus had gone into a snooze and ceased snarling for the night. The snow, which covered the ground, did not help with the search either, and made it even more difficult for the boys to find the opening.

"It's freezing up here!" cried Ian. The boys looked at him and mocked him as if he were a baby, Gamet removing his cloak and placing it over Ian. They used their shields to scoop the snow away and prayed to find some sort of entrance where the sounds had come from.

"It's got to be around here somewhere! We all heard it!" Pike exclaimed.

Laik began to see double, and his head, which he could barely turn, felt as though it was spinning like a windmill. He could still hear Klokus breathing as he closed his eyes to think. He needed to drink. He needed to eat. But the only way to do that was to escape. All of his thoughts and worries took a back seat for once as he grabbed the sole possession he had that was not his weapon; the ashes of Erthos.

He was not sure what it could or would do to him, but it was the only thing besides dirt that he could eat. Laik opened the bottle and looked at it. He figured if he did not try to eat something, he would die anyway, and forced himself up to his knees. Laik scuffled forward, and without realizing exactly how weak he was, he fell to the ground, making enough of a ruckus to awaken Klokus from his nap. Laik quickly opened the bottle and chugged the ashes, the powder-like substance drying his throat and nearly choking him to death. Much like the storm that had formed when Vidion drank his potion, a blizzard began to brew on the mountaintop. This time in the color of green. Klokus now knew where Laik hid and aggressively started to throw the rocks and boulders, which were the only things that protected him, aside.

Up at the top, Odum spotted the green glimmer, which glowed through an area of the snow. The boys ran to it and dug just as quickly as Klokus did with the rocks. The sound from the beast was loud enough to tell the boys that Laik was in trouble, but the blizzard that formed did not make things any easier. The flakes that fell from the sky replaced every scoop of snow they had shoveled away. The four of them held on for dear life as the winds suddenly howled at them and tried to lift them from the ground. Laik had passed out from the pain and choking, but his saliva slowly opened his airway, which allowed him to breathe while he lay motionless.

"I won't stand here and watch. Move!" ordered Gamet as he swung Basher against the crevice, opening a passage large enough for them to get through. Not far inside, they reached their feeble brother and helped each other out of the trap. Gamet took a good look at Klokus, who was rummaging

83

through the final pieces of stone, but the exit they left from was much too small for a beast his size.

After a few moments, the blizzard dwindled to a stop. The mountain was filled with a thick layer of snow, which Gamet enjoyed resting on. He loved the cold and was practically a white fur coat shy of a polar bear. They rested for a few moments to catch their breath, relieved at the fact that Laik was still alive and well. Pike slowly gave him some water, which made him feel better almost immediately, but he was still weak. Laik thanked his friends, and for the first time in days, he was at ease.

The ground began to shake, and the boys all stood up and backed away from the entrance they'd made. It felt as if the source was coming from there. Klokus burst through the ground, and for the first time, all of them got a good look at the creature. The boys stared in terror, and Pike was the first to react. He grabbed his shield and sat on it like a sled, gliding through the snow and the trees. Pike held on to Laik, who was still too weak to defend himself, and the rest of them followed on their shields. The beast chased after them, knocking down trees that stood in his way and crushing every boulder that tried to stop him, but the boys were too fast. They were lucky to escape on their shields, as a heavily wooded area eventually slowed Klokus down enough to lose sight of them.

Gamet reached the bottom first and caught his breath as he lay in the pile of snow he'd landed in. Pike reached it next, still hanging on to Laik, who was also in one piece. Odum came after, and lastly Ian, who nervously yelled, "I'm out! I'm out!"

Ian hadn't noticed he was the last to reach the bottom and looked up the slope for a sign of his friends and the monster. The boys looked at one another and laughed.

84

"We can see that you are out, Ian. You were the last to arrive." Ian looked behind him, his nerves still shaking, and was relieved to see they had all made it.

"...Who made it first?" asked Ian as if it had been a race. In the background, Odum continuously murmured, "Chicken. Chicken. Chicken. Chicken. Chicken."

"Gamet did. Gamet made it down here first...why does that matter?" answered Pike. Ian rolled his eyes, picked up his shield and walked toward them.

"I knew it. I knew it. It had to be his fat ass that sped by all of us with the speed of a runaway boulder." The boys chuckled and continued their journey out of the Grayfalls. Behind them, Klokus still roamed, and the sound of its mighty roar grew closer and closer.

7

Eye of the Beholder

Cold heavy rains fell the rest of the night. The grounds became flooded and swamp-like, and the cold droplets splashed against the top of an encased burial ground. The cold water managed to seep through the cracks and drip down onto Vidion's face. As he awoke, he found himself tied down to a slab made of stone. Weak and weary, he looked around to see if he could recognize the place and then remembered; he had murdered Ghaldon and swallowed the potion. It was the very reason he now found himself tied up. The drink was so potent he'd collapsed, only to be found by a strange-looking woman with a black faded hood over her head. Vidion was not the type of person to allow himself to be caught and imprisoned. Still, he was so frail now that a child could easily control him.

"If you are going to kill me, at least do me the courtesy of bringing me some water," asked Vidion as he tried to break free from the ties and realized the ashes had not made him any stronger. The old woman, who was brewing a strange-smelling mixture, looked over her shoulder.

"I am not going to kill you. I will gladly fetch you some water," she said as she walked toward a small water well that hid in the shadows of a dim corner.

"Then why tie me down like a rabid animal?" he questioned. The old woman walked over to Vidion with a mug of water and helped him drink by lifting his head.

"Because you are violent, Vidion. You are much too strong for someone like me." Vidion swallowed his water and looked at her once more, this time hoping to recognize her face, but the old woman turned around and continued to brew.

"Who are you, and how do you know my name? How do you know who I am?"

"I know quite a bit about everything and everyone... or at least I did. My name is Itola, and at one point in time, people knew me as a prophet, a forecaster, and a seer," she replied. Vidion watched and listened as he waited for further explanation, but Itola seemed to be a woman of few words. The look of impatience on his face was easy to read, and few words were precisely what he did not want.

"Why did you bring me here?" he asked. The woman stopped once again and faced him. She thought for a while as if she were keeping a secret from him and responded, "To help bring you to your full strength."

Vidion began to grind his teeth as he again tugged on the ropes that kept him secured. He found his frustration once again getting the best of him, as he demanded more answers.

"Enough of the games! Why have you chosen me? Why are you helping me? If you were trying to help me, there would be no need to strap me down to this stone... release me, and I will let you live," he demanded as he tried his best to rip through the ropes that kept him tied, but he was still too weak to do anything. "If you are a seer, why do you need me here so bad?

Why did you not leave me where you found me and leave me to die?"

Itola wiped down the stick she used to stir her mixture and placed it down next to the pot. The old woman hobbled over to Vidion, her face still partially covered by her hood and the natural darkness of the burial grounds.

"...Because, Vidion... even though I need you a lot more than you know, you will soon need me as well. I told you. Everyone knew me as a seer. I am the last of my kind." Vidion paused and thought about the benefits of the situation. If she were a seer, that meant she could see the future. He thought to himself that the seer could prove to be more useful than any weapon he had. It would mean he would know what was going to happen before it happened.

"What is it that you need from me? What exactly is it that you could do for me?" questioned Vidion. The old woman smiled at his curiosity and began to loosen the ropes around his ankles and wrists.

"Look at my face, Vidion," she ordered as she removed the hood from over her head and face. "I have three eyes, or at least I'm supposed to. The smallest of the three eyes allow me to see the present; with it, I can see things in the moment. Next in size is the eye of the past. It allows me to look into the eyes of a person and see what haunts them most from their past. I have learned much about people with this eye, and in some ways, I know them better than their loved ones do. The last of my eyes, and the largest of the three, is the eye of the future. Do you see anything odd about it?" she asked sarcastically as Vidion quickly noticed her third eye was missing. Vidion kept his mouth closed and continued to listen. "It was stolen from me, Vidion. Stolen. I spent so much of my life looking into the

88

past and future of others that I never stopped to give myself the chance to see what was in store for me! I focused solely on the wishes and desires of others, no matter what they were, and guided them to happiness!"

The old seer was right. She had spent all of her time helping others with the future. Still, Itola had no consideration for the consequences, either. She helped murderers become murderers, thieves become thieves, and she was even responsible for King Nevil and his reign of tyranny.

"While most would see no weakness or downside to what I have done, I ruined myself the day that I aided King Nevil to the throne. I told him of what was to come, and he used it to become king. That is none of my concern, but what did become my concern was that the king decided I should not be allowed to possess such a gift, the eye of the future. So the following night, King Nevil and his men ambushed me. I never saw it coming because I was too focused on the riches and foods I obtained by allowing desperate men and women to see their future. I was too busy looking into the future of others but never of myself. The King and his men took my eye, but before they yanked it from its socket, I looked. I looked through my future as far as I could, and the very last thing I saw was you. You, Vidion are the one who will help me retrieve my eye."

Vidion laughed with the little strength he had left in him.

"What makes you believe I would? Just because I am now frail does not mean you are my master. I answer to no one, old woman. Do what you must."

"Vidion, I am not telling you to do anything for me. I am asking you, and it is to your advantage. If you retrieve the eye for me, then I will gladly serve you for the rest of my days. I would be able to look into your future and prevent any follies and misfortune before the seeds are ever planted," retorted Itola. Vidion paused for a moment and thought of the possibilities once more. Even though he would soon become as strong as the gods, the seer gave him an advantage that he could only dream of. Vidion was now untied, and sat himself up. He looked over at the old woman, and after some thought, he uttered the words, "If you betray me, Itola, I will take all of your eyes from you; all of them. I will feed them to birds and rip your limbs off. I will make sure you live the rest of your life blind. I will watch you suffer and wither away." Itola smiled and assured him of her loyalty. "I smirk only at the fact that I know you will not be displeased. An eye for an eye, Vidion. If you restore my life to the way it once was, I will ensure your future is even greater." It only took a brief moment for Vidion to agree. He figured he would earn her trust and loyalty by doing her the favor.

"Where should I go? How do I know where to find it?" asked Vidion. The old woman took a few steps back and reached for one of her eyes. When she pulled the eye of the past out, it began to glow like a crystal ball. "Take my eye; with it, you will see the past and see the one who is keeping my third eye in hiding," said Itola. Vidion stared into the orb and watched as the story began to unfold.

In her youth, Itola was exiled from the kingdom and all villages. Still, before forcing her to leave and go into hiding, King Nevil reached for her eye of the future and tore it from its socket. The king used it to his advantage, but soon found that its power was like a double-edged sword. By changing the course of the future to his advantage, he caused a trickle of other events to change as well. Those events resulted in the death of his only daughter. King Nevil searched for the seer for days, but to no avail. Itola was gone, and stayed in hiding until the moment she rescued Vidion. As a result, the king ordered his men to be rid of it, but men are greedy. His knights forced a nearby village to hide it and keep it secret, and from time to time, the knights would use the eye to their own advantage.

Vidion continued to look into the eye of the past and, within moments, learned where it was kept hidden. It was held in a village near Toewood, and Vidion knew precisely where that village was.

"There you see it, Vidion. Bring it to me, and I will help you become the most powerful and feared ruler to ever exist. No one will ever cross you, and no one will ever abandon or betray you the way your family did!" Itola's words undoubtedly grasped his attention and deepest desires. "Your powers are still weak, but I assure you, as time goes by, you will become more powerful than any god that has ever graced this world."

The following morning, Itola woke to find Vidion had left, and she sat with ease, knowing that he headed toward the village to retrieve her eye. After all, it was the last thing about the future that she had seen. Although she was thrilled at the thought of holding her eye once more, she trembled at the fact that the moment in her life when she did not know the future had arrived. The very last thing she foresaw was her eye in Vidion's hand, but for the first time, she feared what would happen to her next.

By this time, Pike and the boys had escaped the Grayfalls and Klokus and settled around a fire. Laik sat silently after he was informed of everything his brother Vidion had done. It was hard for him to accept that his entire family was gone, even more so that it had come about because of Vidion and his betrayal. The boys sat there quietly with him, knowing that there was nothing they could do but stay with him, to help ease his mind.

Odum sat by himself as he mumbled the same usual words to himself, while Gamet sat in silence next to Pike. Pike thought of a way to break the silence but, at the same time, figured Laik would do so when he felt ready. On the ground next to him, he doodled on the soil with a stick he found stuck in his boot. Ian lay face up, staring at the clouds that slowly drifted away from them. At that moment, Ian thought of the heavens, and the possibilities of Laik's loved ones looking down at them. He smiled to himself at the thought and sat up to face Laik.

"I have been holding many of my thoughts back since we got here. I don't know if it's the right time to mention this, but I feel like dwelling in this moment will not help any of us. So I hope you don't mind my words, especially you, Laik." Laik kept his eyes locked on the ground like he had for the past few hours and slowly nodded his head. His eyes were still watery and glossy. "Many people before your grandparents and before us have passed on to another life. Every person that has moved on to another life has left dozens here in our world in mourning. Those people had each other and had their friends, but some of them had no one; no one at all. Although it is a terrible feeling, you are not alone, Laik, and you have us to lean on," said Ian. Laik continued to stare at the ground, analyzing each grain of soil.

"I guess what I'm trying to say is that even though you are going through a tough time, you have us, Laik. We are here for you," Ian continued. Pike smacked his own face in disbelief, wishing that Ian had kept his mouth shut.

"Ian, I am sure Laik knows that. Maybe we should leave him be. We are not going anywhere. He knows that," Pike interjected.

Laik looked up for the first time since they sat down and wiped his tears away. He looked at his friends, and each of them sat up and waited to see what he would do or say.

"It's okay, Pike. Thank you, Ian. I know you mean well, and thank you for your words. I thought I would feel better in silence and sat there quietly, not knowing what to say. But breaking the silence was probably what I needed. You guys are all that I have left," said Laik as his eyes watered once more before he continued. "I am fortunate enough to have four brothers who are here with me right now. All this time, I thought blood made people my family, but I have learned that blood does not matter. Blood proves nothing when it comes to love and loyalty. Vidion fed me lies my entire life, and I believed it because he was my blood. Look at where my faith in him left me. My parents were murdered, my grandfather poisoned, and my grandmother and Iolas burned alive." Ian began to sob as the four brothers gathered around; Gamet placing his hand on Laik's shoulder as if to say 'we are here for you.'

"What kind of gods allow an innocent child... to die? What kind of gods allow the elderly to leave this world in flames and agony?!" yelled Laik. His friends listened as he began to lose faith in the existence of the gods. It was difficult for Pike and Gamet to say anything because they also did not believe in them. Ian, on the other hand, was spiritual, but found himself with no words to defend his belief as he continued to listen to Laik. "The one thing that Vidion didn't lie to me about was exactly that. How could the gods possibly exist when these things happen to good people everywhere? My family didn't deserve this. They didn't deserve to die. Most certainly not the way they died, especially. They were good people. They were honest, and all they ever did was help others!" yelled Laik as he continued to cry.

Ian sympathized with Laik, as the doubt briefly overcame him as well. It was a good question. Why did the gods allow so many good people to die in such terrible ways, and why were people like Vidion and Pike's father, Sid, left here to ravage the world freely? Ian knelt next to Laik and hugged him before speaking.

"I don't know, Laik, but I do know that everything happens for a reason."

Laik rose to his feet, frustrated with Ian's words, which he had heard so many times before, and replied, "And what reason would the gods have for burning my baby brother alive? What reason is there to kill an infant?" Laik balled his fists up as the urge to punch something overcame him. He quickly realized what he was doing and unclenched his fists. He knew Ian meant well, but for the first time, he agreed and sided more with the words of Vidion than with the words of those who loved him most. His thoughts were now parallel with the person he hated most; the last living member of his family.

Laik walked away from them without explanation. The boys looked at one another before Gamet questioned, "Where are you headed to?"

Laik continued walking away as he responded. "I'm going to stop my brother, Vidion."

The boys looked at each other once more as if it were the most absurd idea that ever came from someone's mouth. They rushed toward Laik and stopped him for a moment.

"Wait a second, Laik. Wait," demanded Pike. "We told you what he did. The ashes. He drank the potion. He killed Ghaldon. We saw it with our very eyes. Who knows how powerful he is now? He will be or is the most dominant being in our world, and there is nothing we can do about it." Laik hesitated to mention what he had done himself, but his friends were now his brothers, and his brothers were the only people he felt he could count on.

"I lied to Vidion. I didn't trust him," said Laik. "He spoke to me of his dissatisfaction. He wanted more than becoming a healer and curing our grandparents. He would not have brought your mother back from the dead, even if he could, Pike. I never got to ask him, but it doesn't matter. He only cares for himself. It makes sense now, but for some reason, I chose not to trust him. So I switched one of the ashes that I gave him. I drank the fourth one when I became desperate and weak. I thought I would die if I didn't eat something."

"That explains the green aura we saw before we rescued you," said Pike.

Laik nodded and continued. "I don't know what it will do to me, but if Vidion gains strength from the ashes, then so should I. He will become more powerful than me, yes. But he does not know that I am even alive, much less alive with some of the supposed gods in me. I don't know if the ashes are from the gods or magic that once existed in our world. I do know this, though. I feel stronger. I can feel it in my veins."

Since Laik had only drunk one of the ashes, he was able to regain his strength and health much faster than Vidion. The ashes of Erthos now ran in his blood. Although he was unaware at the moment, the ashes would give him an advantage he could not begin to imagine. His brothers grabbed their belongings and joined Laik in his journey. They walked toward the body of Ghaldon in hope of a sign of Vidion's whereabouts, but there was one thing that they were already too late for. While the boys hiked toward the forest where Ghaldon lay dead, Vidion set foot into the town where the eye of the future was hidden.

8

The Stranger

All was quiet in the village of Mocktoo. Both the men and women had worked relentlessly together after King Nevil's men ravaged the villages a few weeks back. By this time, their homes were finally put back together, and most of the inhabitants had regained their full strength and health. The graves of those who had perished began to sprout the first signs of life, and the crops and gardens they'd planted began to show promise. Vidion, still weak, sat in their tavern and pretended to enjoy a few drinks by himself. He hoped to overhear word of the eye's whereabouts, but that was a secret that had been very well kept for decades. The villagers only spoke of their wishes and ambitions of the near future, which was common among people. Everyone spoke of the things they dreamed of having or doing. Vidion naturally grew tired of the small talk, especially since he knew that the eye was nearby. He knew the eye of the future would be the key to thwart all who would oppose him and all who would come to despise him.

The only useful information he gathered was the fact that the villagers of Mocktoo planned to throw a grand celebration the following night. They were finally finished rebuilding and sheltering all of their townsfolk, and there was nothing Mocktoos liked more than an excuse to celebrate, eat and drink. For Vidion, this was an opportunity. It was an opportunity to use what the seer had shared with him.

The last thing the eye of the past had revealed was that it was kept underground. To be more specific, it was in a secret compartment in a home, which was covered with a uniquely colored carpet. It was crosshatched with textiles of blue, green, and purple, and it had a style that no maker in these lands practiced. Nonetheless, Vidion waited for the festivities to begin for his chance to snoop. The following night, when all of the villagers were out, Vidion crept through each of the homes like a snake preying on mice. Although he did not know which of the houses sheltered the eye, the distinguishable carpet was the one thing he looked for. The memory and image were clear in his mind, and before he knew it, the image seemed to have proved useless. Vidion watched the villagers dance and drink through the windows of their homes, and the moon began to set. The sun started to outline the mountains in the east, which provided extra darkness. Only four of the dozens of homes were left for Vidion to search, and he moved quickly on to the next cottage as the festivities began to fade with the growing sunlight.

All the while, a cloaked rider rode as fast as possible toward the burial ground and the seer's hideout. They stopped several paces away and hugged the horse goodbye. It was almost as if the stranger knew they would never see the horse again and released the creature into the wild. The rider watched as the horse disappeared into the forest, then turned toward the seer's hideout. Once inside, the cloaked figure approached the stone altar and looked at the surroundings. It was as if they knew it would be the last time they laid their eyes on the natural beauties of the world.

The villagers continued their festivities, while Vidion entered the next cottage. He still seemed to be having no luck when, suddenly, the pattern of colors he searched for called out to him from what appeared to be a closet built for extra storage. Vidion dropped to a knee and looked for a compartment or slot where hidden goods could have been stored away. Just as he began his search, the doorknob to the home began to twist open, and Vidion scuttled like a cockroach into the darkness. He quickly concealed himself under a pile of clothing and shoes inside of the large closet and watched through a thin piece of cloth. Vidion kept his breaths short and quiet as he watched a family ready themselves for bed. Suddenly, he began to feel weak and feeble, and the wooziness started to make the room spin. The feeling grew so strong that, in mere seconds, Vidion considered bursting out of the pile of clothes and asking for help, but his pride kept him hidden. He refused to show weakness, and most of all, the thought of failure haunted him.

He regained his composure as best he could, and then he saw it. He spotted a woman with a bracelet that he had seen in the eye of the past. Vidion was now sure that he was in the correct house, and for all he knew, the eye of the future was precisely underneath him. Fortunately for him, a few drunken neighbors came bashing at the front door, and the dwellers ran toward the door, praying that the knocks did not wake their children, who had just fallen asleep. At that moment, the faintness Vidion felt became an ever-increasing pain. The drunks were finally redirected back to their homes, and a roar followed by a thud trembled through their house. The father grabbed a club that hung behind the front door and forced his wife into the room where their kids lay sound asleep. As he crept toward the direction of the thud, Vidion found himself once again waking up after passing out for a few moments from the pain. But this time, he woke up different. He looked at his arms and torso, which appeared to have aged significantly. They looked as if they had nearly doubled in size, and his legs did too. Vidion felt his strength had notably increased as the ashes of the gods rushed through his veins, and listened for the steps that approached him.

The father walked into his room, scanning from left to right. There was nothing out of the ordinary except for the closet door that was now closed. He never closed the door. One of the few things he and his wife argued about was that he always left it open. It was a pet peeve of hers, and he was sure he had not closed it earlier when he grabbed their nightclothes. He pressed his ear against the closet door and listened carefully for a sign of intrusion. It was eerily quiet, the wind from the window overtaking the silence. As if from nowhere, the closet door burst into pieces, sending the father through the air and onto the floor. Out came Vidion, larger and less like a human. He was almost demon-like and without mercy, grabbed the man by his neck and snapped it in two. He looked at him as he watched the life leave his blue eyes, and Vidion tossed his body across the room like a ragdoll and stopped to smell the presence of the man's wife and children. After tearing a hole through the wall, Vidion jumped into the room adjacent to him, and in there, the three remaining family members quivered in fear. It was the last emotion the three of them felt; fear.

Vidion returned to the closet and ripped the carpet off the floor. A hidden latch bolted a small compartment under their home, and in there was a chest. It was easy for Vidion to get into with his brute strength, and there it was; the eye of the future. With the eye in his grasp, he began to witness what the seer could not. The eye displayed the fate of every individual alive, and it overwhelmed Vidion. It was as if he was stricken by all the emotions and anxieties of the world. It was nearly impossible for him to focus until finally, a vision caught his attention. It was him, and he began to focus and think about himself. The eye responded to his thoughts and displayed his future alone. He watched as the eye revealed his rule and dominance, and he grinned at his prosperity. It was the first time in his life when he felt no sorrow and no worry but, then, it was as if the eye presented a word of caution. The eye revealed the seer and her impending predicament. She was shown at the cloaked rider's feet, and if Vidion did not act soon, she would be killed.

"And who might you be? Is there something I could help you with?" asked the seer, who knew nothing of her fate. The stranger nodded and continued to look around. The seer felt uneasy, but tried not to show it. She knew Vidion would return, but hoped he would return soon, as the stranger slowly unsheathed a dagger, still looking at the ruins that stood around them. The stranger took a deep breath, and at long last, after what felt like an eternity to Itola, the stranger spoke.

"I am here to kill you, Itola," she said calmly. "I have seen what the eye of the future says, and it is purely for the greater good. Your eye revealed your plans, and some of the things that you do not know of yet cannot happen. You bring death and destruction, Itola. Your selfishness and willingness to help Vidion will bring more damage to everyone, including you. But it's too late for you to go back. He knows of your power and will now expect it; demand it." The stranger could see a knot in

Itola's throat and tried to ease her mind with more about the future. "It's okay, Itola. I am not here for vengeance or ill will. I, too, will soon be leaving this world. Once Vidion sees that I have killed you, he will kill me. If I run, he will find me. It's what the eye has revealed, and I have accepted it."

The seer became filled with anger. The future was out of her hands, and unless Vidion returned with the eye soon, there was nothing she could do. Instead of showing her rage, however, she tried to stall and replied,

"I understand. If you are going to kill me, would you at least do me the favor of answering one last question for me?" The stranger nodded yes once more. "If you do not kill me, does Vidion rule like the god he was meant to be?" The rider chuckled and answered,

"Vidion will dethrone the king and rule regardless. There is no stopping that... but if I do not end your life, he will never be defeated. You are the key to his eternal success, and even without you, he will succeed."

"... If there is no difference, then why kill me? What difference is it to you to let an old hag like me live?" asked the seer. The stranger walked toward the seer, the dagger still in her hand. As she covered the ground before her, the stranger replied, "If I kill you, one man will stand a chance of stopping him... It is the only chance there is. It is the only chance we all have. I am sorry. Although it is no promise, it is the only chance for a way out." With the last words spoken to the seer, the stranger pierced through her stomach repeatedly. The seer lay silent, and the rider sat on the steps that elevated the altar above ground level. She sat there waiting for Vidion to arrive, knowing that there were only a few more moments left of her life.

Vidion arrived not long after, and could taste the presence

of the stranger. He walked into the entombed burial grounds, and without having to search or fight, the stranger was found sitting patiently in plain sight. The seer's body was on the ground, quiet and motionless. Vidion became enraged at the sight and dropped the eye of the future, which rolled away from his feet. He charged toward the rider, who was now up on her feet and calmly put her palm up, signaling the monster to stop. To her amazement, he did. Vidion stopped right in front of her and roared, waiting for her to speak.

"I know why you have so much hate, Vidion," she said as she removed the cloak and exposed her face to him. It was Elona.

Much of her face was scratched and burned from the fire. The rest of her body was worse than her face, but she held on through the pain and weakness because this was perhaps the most important moment of her life.

"I am sorry to have ruined your plans, my child, but I had to. You are not well, Vidion, and although the eye has shown me what will happen next, I must still plead with you, my boy. I want to help you. Please don't take this path, Vidion. It's not too late. I beg you." Elona dropped to her knees, begging, and at that very moment, the pain overcame Vidion once again.

He dropped to the ground and wriggled in pain, and before he knew it, he was yet again stronger and bigger than before. The ashes were beginning to take effect. His flesh appeared to rot before Elona's very eyes, and the sound of his voice was now beyond recognition. The strength of a sorcerer now seemed to empower him, and Vidion elevated his grandmother from the grounds without a physical touch. She looked into his demon-like eyes and then closed hers. It was now her time, and she knew it. Vidion forced her mouth open and in it he released a drop of his green and poisonous saliva. "You will die before the rising sun." said Vidion, as he released the grip from around her neck. The dose was potent enough to kill, but it would kill her slowly and painfully without an antidote.

Elona lay on the ground, wounded. Despite everything that had happened, Elona smiled at her oldest grandson and whispered, "I love you." Vidion looked into her eyes as if her words and actions meant nothing. Then, from the corner of his eye, he spotted movement from the seer who happened to utter his name. The eye of the future had rolled to her when Vidion dropped it on the ground, and in desperation to learn her fate, she saw that she would die. But with that, she learned of a vital clue that would help Vidion. Her strength was now leaving her as she called for Vidion to come closer.

"You will become more powerful than the gods, Vidion," she struggled to say, as her last few breaths were upon her. "No one will be able to stop your rise as our master, but you must be cautious. Your brother still lives. He will be the one to stop you unless you kill him first... He took it, Vidion... He took it... " The seer spoke of the ashes of Erthos. It was one of the last things she saw besides Vidion's doom. Vidion grew frustrated at the fact that the seer was now fading away. It was already angering enough for him to learn that his brother was still alive, and he would be the one to ruin him. The seer tried to mention something his brother took, but before he could get it out of her, her body turned to ash, along with the eyes.

9

The Murky Path

The curse on the haunted forest was finally lifted after centuries of eerie happenings and the disappearance of many people. The fog and mist slowly began to dissipate, but for the moment, it was still thick enough to cloud their perception and lengthen their search for Ghaldon's remains. A vast amount of energy was still present, and remnants of the purple storm bolted from tree to tree. The boys were lucky not to get hit by any of the remaining bolts as they retraced their footsteps toward Ghaldon and his den.

Upon returning, what was left of the den was set afire with purple flames that blushed through the mist. Laik entered the hole and learned nothing of Ghaldon or Vidion, but soon became informed of the type of magic and sorcerous power he was up against. Scattered throughout the ground were books of different muted colors. It was as if each color had a purpose. Several of the books were ripped and spread throughout the lair. They appeared to be books of spells and demons or monsters that once roamed their world. It was either that or the beasts still existed, but Laik paid no mind and continued to look for hints. Gamet entered the den and collected as many of the books as could fit in his satchel. They were intriguing to him, and he gathered as many of the different colors as he could. Ian stood guard and looked around as best as he could through the mist and the trees. He jolted at every twig that cracked or owl that screeched, but tried his best to stay on guard and not show his brothers that he was afraid. He had a reputation for being fearful of everything, but his brothers did not care. They loved it at times. They loved to tease him and poke fun at his fear because it was an easy target and a great laugh. The only thing they found easier were jokes about Gamet and his plumpness.

While the rest of the boys stuck to their duties, Pike could not help but notice a large rock in the distance. Although it was difficult to see through the fog, this rock stood out because it was significantly darker than the other stones, which appeared to be gray. Pike walked toward the black rock with his hatchets out, careful to avoid attacks from an animal or monsters from the books. Pike nudged the rock with his boot, and to his surprise, it was not a rock at all. It was the remains of Ghaldon, which were mostly cloth and bone. Lodged into Ghaldon was Vidion's weapon, which Pike recognized. Pike called for his brothers, who all came rushing with their weapons drawn. Even though Ian was the one they usually made fun of for being a coward, they all secretly felt afraid of the forest and what was in it. After all, they'd all spent many years listening to the myths and tales about these haunted lands.

Even though most of them had witnessed the slaying, it was odd for them to be near the body of a sorcerer. It was the first time reality hit them all. It was the first time they realized that the issue at hand was not about a kid's game, a stupid dispute, or a name that someone called someone else. It was a life or death situation, and the foe was someone they were familiar with; Laik's brother. The boys spotted a set of footprints, which led away from Ghaldon. They had to have been Vidion's, because there was no one else around when Ghaldon was killed. Step by step, they followed the tracks deeper into the forest until the steps finally came to a halt. The outline of a body was smudged into the dirt. It appeared that Vidion might have fallen or laid on the ground. The imprint of his body then appeared to have been dragged. Then, as the boys neared the end of the trail, they came across the burial ground where the seer lived.

Laik entered the cavern-like tomb with caution, and his brothers followed closely behind him. All of them still had their weapons drawn, and the eerie silence of the grave was the only thing they could hear. As they entered the room where the altar stood in the center, a single drop of water landed on Laik's shoulder. Then he recalled. His grandmother used to tell him stories about the drops of water that occasionally fell on people whenever they wandered through a cave. She used to call them cave kisses, and she would always tell Laik that if someone received a cave kiss, it would bring good fate, love, and prosperity. Laik smiled at the thought, but the feeling soon came to a halt with the sight of two bodies on the ground. Ian and Laik ran toward the nearest one and carefully tried to turn the body around. It was all ash and bone, and these were the remains of the seer. Then Pike, Gamet, and Odum yelled the terrible words, which they wished they did not have to say.

"Laik! It's your grandmother! Elona! She's alive!"

Laik's heart sank and he sprinted toward his grandmother. She was shivering and desperately holding on to the final moments of her life.

"I was told you were dead! How did you get here? What's

wrong?" questioned Laik as he frantically tried to make her feel better. Elona stopped his efforts and asked him to listen carefully.

"My beautiful grandson. I have been poisoned, and you must listen to me before I go." All of the boys' eyes began to water as they continued to listen. "I always told you not to worry about me, yet I always knew that this moment would come. I never told you about Itola's eye, the eye of the seer. It now exists as part of a pile of ashes; over there," said Elona as she pointed at the seer's remains. "I could not tell you what I knew because if I did, the future would have changed. A chain of events would have occurred, which would have doomed us all forever. The eye was an advantage we had. It showed me the future, Laik, and now only the ones in this room will know. You will be the one to stop your brother. The eye of Itola revealed it. Vidion will be stopped by his brother." Elona cleared her throat, which was filled with blood. Laik's thoughts raced with a thousand questions, but he tried his best to maintain his composure and save his grandmother.

The boys forced Elona to save her strength and carried her out of the tomb. There was an herb in Toewood that worked especially well for those who were poisoned, but time was not exactly on their side. The hike to the remnants of Toewood would take longer than the rising sun. Halfway to their home, Elona asked to be placed on the ground. She began to spew the contents of her stomach, which was mostly blood. Laik held her so that she would not feel alone, but Elona knew that it was the end for her.

"You must stop him, my boy. He aims to bring death to us all; the human race. Everything that everyone worked so hard for and every precious moment that ever existed will be erased unless you stop him. It would be as if you never existed, your grandfather and myself as well. I don't want our memories to die, Laik," said Elona.

"Let's talk about something else grandma. Don't speak of death. You're not going to die. Tell me about the tree. You never had a chance to tell me about the tree. The one that doesn't exist any longer," cried Laik as he tried to catch his breath and get Elona to change the subject.

"Ah yes. The tree," replied Elona with a smile. "They were known as Oakin trees, and they were forbidden to be touched. Folklore says that the gods put them here to help shield us. Their leaves were a source of power and protection, but the gods witnessed how greedy men could be. The gods knew that a sword like The Bloodstone could be forged in the wrong hands, and so, they took the Oakin trees with them as they disappeared into the heavens. The..."

Elona's eyes began to roll back before she could finish her story, and Laik's heart sank. In a final effort to get his grandmother the herbs she needed to live, Laik picked her up on his shoulders and ran toward their hometown. The murky weather and steep terrain was just too much for anyone to travel through, and the boys soon found themselves having to stop to catch their breath yet again. They each took turns trying to carry Elona, but even that was too exhausting. It was impossible and, before they knew it, the sun was starting to rise.

Laik wiped away his tears and hugged his grandmother, and with her final breaths, Elona whispered her last words.

"Take this," she said while handing him a uniquely shaped leaf. "It was pulled from the last Oakin tree to exist. May its beauty remind you of me, and its imperfections remind you that life is not perfect, but it is worthwhile. I love you, my child.

Keep it for as long as you can."

The boys carried Elona's body the rest of the way and allowed Laik to mourn. They buried her in Toewood in an area in which she had loved to spend time and relax. Pike, Ian, Odum, and Gamet struggled to maintain their composure, because Elona was like a grandmother to them. But naturally, Laik was distraught. He sat on a fallen tree trunk and observed a pair of ants that appeared to be in a hurry. A few feet away, the ants reached another who seemed to be dying, and carried him on their backs. Laik continued to observe as the ants brought their friend into their colony, and then he smiled for a moment. He smiled at the thought of his own friends, and how he was sure they would do the same for him. Laik wiped away his tears and helped his brothers finish burying his grandmother. In fear of having her remains dug up, they marked her grave with a few distinctively shaped stones. The five of them stood there in silence as they remembered the good moments and all of the things Elona had done for them.

"The sky is about to fall on us, boys. Heavy rains. We should seek shelter for the night," suggested Gamet. They stayed under a large tree near the grave and tried their best to sleep, despite the horror of the past few days. None of them spoke a word until the following morning when, without a bite to eat, the five of them headed back to the tomb. They reached the crypt by nightfall, but the hunger and exhaustion put them right to sleep. Around midnight, a few cockroaches made their way into the area where the boys slept. If there was anything besides fat people that Gamet disliked, it was cockroaches. Luckily, Gamet was in a deep sleep and was snoring loudly with his mouth open. The roaches took their time, but eventually found themselves on Gamet's chest. Laik happened to wake up and witness them climb onto Gamet and snickered at the thought of his reaction to the roaches. Gamet was terrified of them. Laik continued to watch as one of them made its way into Gamet's mouth. Its legs trampled all over his lips, and Gamet immediately spat the creature out. To Laik's surprise, Gamet did not yell and quietly regained his composure without waking any of the boys. Naturally, he could not fall back to sleep as he looked over every inch of the room for more of the roaches. Laik laughed to himself, careful not to let Gamet know that he had seen what had happened, and crushed the bugs with his thumb after Gamet walked away. He had been kissed by a roach, and he could not believe it. The thought of it replayed in his mind, and every time it did, he could feel the creature's legs pressed against his tongue. Gamet walked toward the altar in the center of the room and took the few steps up.

After inspecting the altar for cockroaches, Gamet leaned against it with all of his weight. After some time, the thought of the roaches finally left his mind, but just as the thoughts cleared, the altar shifted to the side, and Gamet went tumbling down a set of hidden steps. "Oh, shiiit!" he yelled. The boys woke to the sound of his squawk, and the only thing they saw was the passage that Gamet had accidentally revealed. They quickly gathered their things and ran down the steps to meet their brother. Gamet was fine and was up on his feet by the time they reached the bottom, but right before them was a path, which led away from the tomb.

The boys followed the path with no incident except for a few scares. In the end, the trail led outdoors, and not far from the exit stood the remains of a very old temple. It appeared it had been there for centuries. The structure was immaculate, and the like of that which the boys had only heard of in Elona's stories.

Then they saw it; the symbol of the gods; and behind it was the shrine of Zalia. They entered and admired its beauty, and for a brief moment, everything felt okay to Laik. He felt a sense of inner peace and thought that, just maybe, his grandmother was indeed in a better place, and not in an empty black abyss.

Then the skies became dull. Yet another storm hovered over them, and although the thunder cracked unusually loud, the purple strikes of lightning did not easily perplex them. It was a sign that Vidion was near, and in the distance, on top of a hill, a figure gazed back at them.

"It's Vidion," Pike thought out loud as he looked through a window. The boys stepped outside of the temple through the back door. Through the night sky and the winds, Vidion spoke to them.

"I have waited a long time for a moment like this. Our parents chose you over me, and for the past fourteen years, I had to watch you, care for you, and pretend to love you while I had to watch you take my place. I was pushed away and forced to wait for my very own mother to remember that I still existed. Now you will be the one to wait. You will watch your loved ones leave you one by one. Your death will come by my hand, and you will live the rest of your days not knowing when. You will learn what true fear is as you count each day in sheer panic. Today, one of the ones you call brother will die. You will learn how it feels to go through life with no one, just like I did."

Vidion disappeared into the night, but before he did, what sounded like a spell or curse drifted through the skies in a language unknown. The boys stood ready and on guard, but nothing happened. Ian and Pike took a few moments to ease Laik's mind, who was finding himself with a tightened chest and shortness of breath. His fear of death was the only thing that ever deterred him and prevented him from living a normal life, and his brothers knew it. The five of them hiked in the direction of the hill and not even a thousand paces in, they came across what seemed to be old farming land. It stretched to the foot of the hill, and none of the ground supported life or crops the way it used to. In some areas, it resembled wetland more than farmland.

The land was old and useless. On a regular day, the grounds dried up like a raisin, but the skies had been heavy the past few days, and the water was shin-deep in some areas. Other parts were deep enough for a grown man to drown in, but thankfully, each of the boys knew how to swim. The most challenging part of crossing the field was a thick layer of fog that hovered just above the water. It was thick enough to prevent them from seeing past their waistline, but it was not the hardest part mentally. Scattered throughout the field, the remains of large wooden posts stood, tall, yet rotten. Some of them were tilted to the side, which made them even eerier, but what caught the boys' eyes were not the posts. Some of the posts still had the decrepit remains of scarecrows, which were once used to protect the farmland. It was as if they were watching over the terrain. The boys stayed close to one another, especially Ian, who was already nervous about entering the mist as it was.

Nearly halfway across the field, the water became thick with mud, and their steps became more of a swish through the mud. It became difficult to trot along, as they often found themselves tripping and stumbling on large rocks and ditches. Still, as always, the boys found the humor in the terrible situation. Gamet seemed to be struggling the most, since he was a bit on the heavy side. Every few seconds, his face met the mud, and every time he did, the boys burst out laughing. They even admitted to peeing in their pants out of laughter, because it did not matter. They were all covered in worse things, and the water helped wash away the urine away anyway. Gamet began to use every excuse he could for his clumsiness. Still, even he knew he was struggling with his weight and eventually admitted his defeat.

Pike wiped away the tears of laughter and tried to relax his cheeks, which were hurting from laughing so much. Once the blur of tears subsided, he noticed a figure rush into hiding behind a shrub. The look on his face worried the boys who, without question, listened to Pike's instructions.

"Act normal," said Pike. "Someone is following us. I just watched them run behind a shrub. Gamet, push me to the ground." Gamet looked at him with a confused face.

"What?" "Push me to the ground, Gamet! You guys laugh at me, and I am going to crawl over there under the fog to get them." Gamet shoved Pike as hard as he could with pleasure, and a genuine chuckle came out of all of them, except Laik. He was still in shock and disbelief, and all he could think about was getting to Vidion. Pike crawled closer and closer to the shrub, disappearing into the mist, and his heart began to race faster and faster the closer he got. The boys continued to act as if Pike were at their feet, but waited for his signal, and once Pike reached the spot, he popped out from the mist with his hatchets drawn. Pike froze for a moment as he was sure he witnessed someone hide behind it. He circled the shrub and poked his foot through the thick fog, desperately hoping to hit and stop whatever it was that he had seen.

The boys watched closely as Pike exhausted himself and came to a stop. Naturally, they began to tease him, and Pike now became the joke and new person to make fun of. Gamet took full advantage and began to yell, "What a wimp!"

Ian, on the other hand, had more to say because he rarely had the opportunity to make fun of Pike. "You know... I may be afraid of my own shadow...but at least I'm not afraid of my imaginary friend, Pike." For the first time, Gamet and Odum joined him in laughter, and it was, for once, not at him.

"Eat my balls," cried Pike. The boys continued to tease him, and at that precise moment, the figure quietly began to rise from the mist. He rose behind Pike and was now clearly visible. It was one of the scarecrows that appeared to have come alive. Laik watched speechlessly, but in his mind, he realized that Vidion's foreign words must have been a spell, a spell on the scarecrows.

"Pike... there is a living scarecrow behind you. Come now. Calmly," said Gamet.

"Suck my butt," responded Pike, who was now convinced that his friends were only teasing him.

Laik realized Pike was not going to take them seriously after the teasing he had just endured, and came forward.

"Pike...it's not a joke," said Laik. Pike now had a knot in his throat after hearing the words from Laik, and as he turned to face the figure, the scarecrow shrieked an ear-piercing sound; his mouth filled with flames from the inside.

The boys ran for their lives. The scarecrow was large, but struggled to walk through the mud just as they did. Every turn the boys made proved to be useless in their escape. It was mostly because another and yet another scarecrow rose from the mist and aimed to kill them. Each of the scarecrows had claws, but they were unlike anything they had ever seen. The claws were long and flaming, and every swing they took set the few dry shrubs and grasses on fire. Still, the fog buried their steps, and the boys soon found themselves unexpectedly rolling down what felt like a hill. The fog hid the slope, and made it appear as if the land was leveled with the foot of the hill. Instead, the foot of the hill was deep under the mist. The boys were now under a sea of haze and soon came to a stop at the very bottom. The scarecrows knew the lands very well and carefully walked down the slope in search of their prey.

Laik and the rest of them could see their eyes, their mouths, and their claws burning red through the thick fog. In the direction of the hill, a large shelter appeared to be the best chance for escape. They quickly ran inside and hid wherever they could. Odum dove into a mound of hay and buried himself as best as he could, while Pike sought the higher ground and balanced himself on a wooden support beam. Ian quickly closed himself into an oak barrel, and then there was Gamet, who was too heavy and too big to hide anywhere he could see. In desperation, Gamet climbed a ladder, which led to the same support beams that Pike was standing on. The beam creaked under his weight, and Pike signaled at him to stop. Gamet froze on the spot and balanced himself using a pillar. Laik, on the other hand, ran out of time and, instead, concealed himself behind an unhinged door that leaned against the wall. He watched as the scarecrows entered the shelter. Out of all of the things that ran through his mind, he noticed that one of the scarecrows' eyes was apparently extinguished. Smoke seeped from its socket as if water had splashed on its face, and this gave Laik an idea which was now the only plan of escape that Laik had. He had to somehow drench them and put out the flames.

Hanging on the support beams was an enormous container. The container was filled after days of rain, and its contents dripped from the cracks that time had created. The scarecrows scavenged through the area in search of the boys, and Laik continued to watch. As one of them neared the dripping water, a few drops landed on its shoulder. It let out a horrible screech as if it was being burned, and then it clicked in Laik's mind. Their bodies were made of nothing but rotting wood, but what brought them to life were the cursed flames on the outside. Laik carefully crept over to a pile of debris as he quietly began to sneak his way up to the beam. It was cracking where the container hung, and both Gamet and Pike began to slowly walk off it before it snapped.

Laik continued to sneak past the scarecrows, who were now on full alert. They carefully walked through the shelter in search of the boys, and then their attention was turned toward the barrel where Ian hid. Out of sheer fear, Ian pooped in his pants and, in the process, passed gas as loud as one could imagine. The smell of his gas was enough to make his eyes tear up, and if that was not enough to give himself away, he began to gag at the smell.

The scarecrows all gathered around the barrel and raised their flaming claws. Gamet, Pike, and Laik watched in terror, and each of them tried to think quickly to help their brother escape. Just before they could act, however, Odum burst out of the haystack and yelled, "Odum!" The scarecrows directed their attention toward him, and the yell was so loud, it startled both Pike and Gamet. Gamet lost his balance and fell on the beam. His weight was too much for the shaft, which was already stressed and cracked in half. Down went both of them along with the container, and the scarecrows were doused in water. Their cries were so loud the boys had to cover their ears and watch as the scarecrows' flames came to an end. The fire proved to be their source of life as their charred wooden bodies lay lifeless on the ground. The boys looked at one another and jumped for joy.

"Gamet! For once, your fatness helped us!" yelled Pike, who hugged him even though they had both had a very painful fall and landing. Ian opened the barrel, utterly oblivious to the fact that he had nearly been killed, and he had Odum to thank.

"You, Ian, can thank Odum. The scarecrows were practically at your throat after they heard your butt juice squeeze through your crevice. When Odum yelled, it was to get them away from you. To be fair... I almost soiled myself as well," explained Gamet.

For a few moments, Laik forgot about his grandmother and cracked a smile as he watched Pike, Ian, and Gamet hug Odum. Odum never spoke more than a few words, but his actions always spoke loudly. He loved them and always made sure that his friends were okay. The boys picked up their belongings and headed toward the exit. It was now barricaded by the debris that had followed the beam.

"Chicken," Odum proclaimed, as he walked toward the rubble and tossed it aside. The boys made their way toward the foot of the hill, which was now only a few paces away.

Odum looked around at the foggy field and took the lead, Laik behind him, and the rest of them followed. The fog seemed to grow thicker as they neared the hill; their sight, even more than before, hindered from the waist down. And then, within the blink of an eye, despite their caution and careful steps, yet another scarecrow abruptly rose from the haze, attacking Odum. Laik reacted quickly and with his sword hacked at the scarecrow's wooden lower half; its body splashed into the water and withered away with a loud screech. Startled, the boys drew their weapons and looked around at their surroundings, searching for more of the evil spirits that were after them. The flames from another one of their claws caught their attention, but before attacking, they noticed that the claws were not moving. They was still, and it was as if the claws were staring at them. They did not even twitch, which was odd for such an aggressive creature. The boys approached with caution, still with a watchful eye. The fog was much too thick to see the entire creature, but the closer they got, the clearer they were able to see. It was Odum, and the claws of the scarecrow they'd just gotten rid of were embedded into his chest. Odum was on the ground gasping for air, and the boys quickly and carefully picked him up, despite his large size, and placed him on a boulder that was at a level with the mist.

"Hang on, Odum. Hang on. We will... we will get you help. We will... get you home," said Laik, who knew very well that by the time they did get back home, it would be too late, not to mention the fact that Toewood was destroyed and everyone who lived there was gone. Before they knew it, Odum turned pale and cold to the touch. He began to shiver, and before he took his last breath, he uttered his final words. "Seven... Seven."

For the first time in a long time, the boys all felt alone and helpless. They knew there was nowhere to go and no one to turn to. Their families and homes were burned to the ground, and the promise that Vidion had made was beginning to take place. Laik's dear friend Odum was gone. Death became the last thing that Laik remembered about his childhood. Despite all of the great moments of his youth, the ones that clung in his memory were the ones where he found himself having to say goodbye to those he loved.

10

Aroku

In a tavern not far from the misty field, a group of men began to argue and brawl over the last of the ale. The town faced a shortage of supplies, much like every other town, but their scarcity was mostly of ale. While the men practically fought to the death for a drink that would kill them slowly anyway, Sid, Pike's father, took advantage of the situation and chugged the last beer. He reached over the counter and grabbed the drink, while the server tried his best to stop the arguing and brawling. Sid did not show an ounce of remorse and jumped out of the tavern's back window. He savored the drink, which mostly foamed on his beard. After placing his eye patch over his blind eye, Sid walked into the woods, where he had remained out of sight since the murder of his wife.

He crunched through the dead leaves for hours, and then from one moment to the next, he suddenly felt a presence. Someone was watching him. Sid quietly snuck out a sword and pretended not to hear or notice anything as he continued to enjoy the crunching sound of the leaves. He looked around with his peripheral vision, but he could only see so much with one eye. As he turned a corner, which was hidden by shrubs, Sid hid behind a thick tree trunk.

A towering figure followed his footsteps and sniffed around for his scent. Sid figured it was likely the owner from the tavern who'd realized he had left without paying. As the figure came closer, Sid jumped out from behind the tree with the intent to kill him, but he froze. He suddenly felt all of his muscles squeeze together and became as stiff as the tree he had hidden behind. Sid was unable to blink even, and if it were not for a strange force that kept him propped up, he would have bashed his face against the hard roots of the tree that swelled from the ground. As the figure came closer and stepped into the moonlight, Sid recognized his face and gasped. It was Vidion, except Vidion had nearly doubled in size, and his face and skin appeared foul. He looked more like a demon than a human, and it was the first time Sid had come across such a beast.

Vidion released him, and after he filled his lungs back up with air, Sid swung his sword at Vidion, aiming to chop off his head. To Sid's bewilderment, Vidion turned his sword into ashes, and Sid once again found himself defenseless on the ground.

"If you attempt my life again, I will make sure you end up like your sword," promised Vidion.

"You were nothing but a bastard boy. How did you do that?" asked Sid, still confused and curious to know how he had turned the sword to ash and lifted him in the air without a single touch.

"Gods do not exist, Sid, but there are certain wonders in our lands that do. They come in the likes of enchantments and curses. I am the result of them." Sid smirked and slowly rose to his feet.

"You're a sorcerer? Is that what you're saying, Vidion?"

"...And future King... but every great ruler needs someone to carry out his deeds. Every great ruler needs someone who will make sure things get done. I want that to be you," answered Vidion. Sid thought for a few moments, dumbfounded at the fact that Vidion wanted him to help, of all people. Sid had never harmed a hair on his body, but he'd never done anything for him either.

"Why me? Is this some kind of set-up?" asked Sid. Vidion was still weak, and limped closer to reply.

"Because you are the only person I know who would be willing to do the things I am going to ask. You are the only person I know who will be willing to forget about what is right or wrong and do what is necessary. I watched you as I grew into the man I am today, and I think it was brave of you to do what you did to your family. It had to be done for your sake; for your contentment." He reached out and hovered the palm of his hand over Sid's blind eye. Vidion uttered a spell to cure him, and within seconds, Sid regained sight in his eye. The only thing that remained was a scar across his face and eye socket.

Sid looked around in disbelief. He had been sure that he would never see from his eye again, but thanks to an enchantment from a young man he considered a worthless boy, he was able to see again. Sid knelt to showcase his allegiance to the sorcerer, but honor and loyalty were not in his interest. He knew that with such a powerful being at his side, he would become practically invincible. Running Vidion's errands, no matter what they were, was surely worth it in his mind. "I am yours to command, Vidion. What would you like me to do?"

"It is only a matter of time until I gain my full strength, but until then, I cannot engage against a whole army. My body will become weak, and King Nevil's guards will spear me to my demise. You, on the other hand, can manipulate people like no other. It was one of the things I admired about you growing up. I plan to overthrow the king and take his place, but I must rid the world of any blades, spears, and weapons that were forged of steel. They are the only weapons I cannot withstand, and the knights will become powerless, the villagers even more. No one on this planet will have the strength or weapons to defeat me. Before they know it, I will have them all in cages, serving me with my every desire. I will feed them just enough to live and carry out my cause. The weak and the old will be sentenced to death. You, Sid, will work by my side. You will have whatever it is that you want as long as you do what is asked."

Sid smiled and rose from the ground. Still ecstatic with the return of his vision, he questioned, "So what's your plan, Master?"

"I have the power to turn them all to ash, like I did to your sword, but I need one thing. I need the sword of the king. For this spell to work, I must possess the eldest of kings' swords. King Nevil holds the oldest sword that exists. It was passed on from generation to generation, and with it, kings and their armies will not stand a chance against myself and my horde."

Typically, Sid did not work with anyone, but this was too good of an opportunity to pass. Vidion explained the plan as they traveled toward King Nevil's castle. Before they knew it, Sid approached the front gates of the stronghold with a carriage attached to two horses.

"I must see the King! I am from the village of Andima, and there is a disease that is spreading like wildfire! It has spread to two of the villages near us, and I have reason to believe it is coming from the water. The river! I have proof here!" Sid jumped off of the carriage and revealed the putrid skin on Vidion's leg. He was wrapped from head to toe as if he were a deceased body. The king's men were stunned after seeing the size of Vidion. They urgently sent the message to the king, and before long they escorted Sid to the king's hall; the guards transporting the body right behind him. The body was placed at the foot of the king's throne. Sid knelt and lowered his head for permission to speak.

"What is this disease you speak of? Why are you so sure it stems from the water in your town?"

"My Lord, I serve my townsmen as a messenger. I deliver all of their needs, and I see things others do not, since I travel so often. I have noticed many of the villagers with the same symptoms, one of which I brought here for you to see for yourself," Sid explained as he uncovered Vidion's body before continuing. The king looked at his rotting flesh and gagged at the sight.

"I believe the source of this disease is from the Kolino River. I have watched the villagers return from there extremely ill, and their families soon after. They all end up looking like the body I have brought before you. The villages near the waterway to the south have shown no symptoms. I have come to you because I know your men retrieve water wherever they please. I do not want this to spread even further."

The king showed his gratitude and tossed Sid a few coins like a beggar and sent his guards to alert his knights. Once they had gone, Sid rose from his knee, walked toward the doors of the hall and locked them.

"What are you doing? Unlock that door at once before I have your head cut off!" demanded the king. Vidion sat up slowly and turned his head toward the king. Only two of his knights were on guard in the hall with him, and Vidion crushed their armor and the guards within it. Vidion hobbled over to the king and struck him across the face. The guards that were locked out rang the bells to warn all knights of the invasion, and the king's men rushed toward the great hall. King Nevil shook off the pain and drew the sword that Vidion needed. With it, King Nevil prepared to defend himself and the kingdom. "I am the king because people fear me. I have not been overthrown because the people respect me and know that I will do whatever is necessary to keep our lands safe and free of people like you! Draw your sword, you bastard! You will regret the day you dared strike a king!"

Vidion did not have a sword, because his ego told him he was too mighty for a blade, but the gauntlets that were wrapped around his forearms were made of steel. He used them as a shield with every strike the king made against him. All the while, the knights tried to quickly bang down the massive doors to the hall. Sid began to struggle with a few of the knights who had entered through a back entrance to the room. Sid barely gained control of the opening, but using a torch that hung on the wall, he set the back entrance and its door ablaze. The knights were forced to travel back downstairs and to the front entrance, where the large doors were by now nearly open. Vidion had soon grown tired; he had underestimated King Nevil and his ability to defend himself and the kingdom. King Nevil was great with a sword and kept in shape by practicing every day.

Vidion dropped to the ground, his body weak from both the struggle and the potion. He was almost sure he had failed and lowered his head in hope of a swift and painless death.

"Let this serve as a lesson to you and anyone else who ever dares think about trying such a treacherous act against me again. The bones I have down in the cellar belong to the graves

124

from your home. They were rats, all of them, and your remains will be thrown there with the rest," said King Nevil as he raised his sword, but before he was able to chop off the head of the snake, Sid charged at the king, whose sword tumbled out of his hands and on to the ground. Vidion tried to regain his strength as the two struggled on the ground, and at that same moment, the knights burst through the door.

"Don't move. Nobody come closer!" demanded Sid as he pressed the edge of his knife against the king's throat. "One step closer and I will slice his throat wide open." The knights looked at each other, confused as to what to do as the king requested them to lower their weapons calmly. Vidion watched with high approval as Sid took control of the situation. By now, he had caught his breath again. Both of them cautiously backed out of the room, with King Nevil as their hostage. In his mind, Vidion had planned on exiting the castle, but Sid was much older and much more experienced in the life of crime.

"Let's head down to the cellars," suggested Sid. "They will be swarming the land looking for us, but they will not expect us to stay on their grounds. Let's go to the cellar and finish what you are here to do." Once again, Sid gained Vidion's approval, and the three of them headed toward the cells. Most, if not all, guards were on high alert and left the town in search of their king. The ones who stayed guarded the entrance, and others kept a watchful eye in the tallest of towers.

The three of them snuck their way down into the cells with the guidance of the king. A knife against his throat was enough to convince him, but even though he cooperated with their demands, the king felt assured that the two of them would be caught.

"You cannot get away with this. You will be found, and you

will be burned alive," said King Nevil. Vidion once again struck him across the face, this time with his forearm, which was covered by his steel gauntlets. The strike opened a gash above his eyebrow, blood trickling down his face. King Nevil looked at him with great fury as Vidion chained him to the wall. Vidion grabbed the king's sword and analyzed it. "It is said that with the eldest of swords in my hand, I have the power to incinerate all weapons of steel. Yours has been passed from generation to generation and has existed since the gods roamed these lands, I heard. Tonight, your army will fall. Your kingdom will crumble, and your people will suffer."

The King watched in both anger and horror as Vidion leaned his blade against the wall. Vidion walked toward Nevil and stared at him face to face. And then, without uttering a word, Vidion grabbed his face and nearly twisted his neck off. The king's body fell on the ground and hung from the chains that strapped him against the wall. Vidion grabbed the aged sword, and with it in his grasp, Vidion closed his eyes and spoke the words of magic. All around the kingdom armor, blades, and steel turned to ash, including his very own gauntlets. The air became filled with ash, and those who inhaled it choked to death as it burned their lungs from the inside. The sword of the king was now the only sword to exist, which Vidion kept as his own.

The knights of King Nevil frantically continued their search for the king with whatever they could find to defend them. Before long, the body of King Nevil was discovered in the cellar. It was thrown on the ground. Sid and Vidion hid behind the cellar doors, and once the guards entered, the doors were shut, trapping the guards inside with them. Sid readied himself with a drawn bow and arrow, which he'd found in a room of old weapons near the cells. The guards attacked at first sight. Most, if not all, of the knights' weapons, were old wooden shields and the wooden shafts of their spears as well, but every swing and thrust was useless against someone as powerful as Vidion. The power he'd gained from Flonius' ashes would burn and melt the wood away. Clubs that were set afire would be useless, as the water from Wyolus would extinguish the flames upon contact with Vidion's body. And the knights that would be lucky enough to reach Vidion would be blown away by the gusts of Airos or shot by Sid and his arrows. Vidion was nearly invincible, but the one part he did not have and the one part he was unaware of was running strong through Laik's veins. It was the ashes of Erthos. Nonetheless, all of the land was now Vidion's.

"All those who oppose me will be executed. For those who kneel to my name, keep them. Have them help you in our undertaking. You will go from village to village and imprison the others. We will build great forts with enough cages to hold them all, and they will all be separated. Fathers will no longer stand with their children as my father failed to stand by me. They will be worked to death without food or drink. The men with no children will be allowed to live so long as they swear their allegiance to me. They will be used as slaves as well, but keep them alive. The women will be kept alive as well, but they will not be shown any respect. They will be used for the benefit of men. They will pay for their betrayal, like my mother's betrayal of me when my brother came into this world. And the children... they will raise one another. They, too, will be kept disconnected from man and woman. They will be kept away to force both men and women to continue serving me."

Sid was enthralled with Vidion's plan, but he could not help but remain concerned at the fact that he had no one to help him see the deed through.

"Master... I ask with the utmost respect. How would you suggest I complete this task with everyone in a cage?"

Vidion closed his eyes, and like a voice inside of Sid's head, the foreign words of a spell echoed throughout the great hall. Vidion dropped to a knee once more, still not at his full strength, and asked Sid to look through the window. To Sid's astonishment, lava began to ooze from the ground and seep into the moat that surrounded the castle. The moat soon dried over, and after a few moments, a horde of monsters began to surface. They were called the Aroku, and they were mostly stone and rock, but at the core was the magma that kept them alive. Sid smirked at the fact that he was in control of the newly found legion, and with them, he began to bring Vidion's plan to life. No one was able to stop them, and Vidion's idea came to fruition not long after. Worst of all, his strength had finally grown in full. The skies and clouds gloomed with different shades of gray and purple, mostly above the castle. It was a sign of what was to come, and the darkest and gloomiest days were now about to begin.

II

Part Two

11

Leaflake

Deep beneath the moat, the magma had nearly depleted itself with the continuous formation of Aroku. Most of the trench and castle was obsidian by now, which gave it its eerie, black, glossy appearance. There were four main pits from which the Aroku rose.

After nearly twenty years, hordes of them wandered through the lands in search of villagers who escaped capture. Half of the Aroku roamed through the halls of the castle, and the other half either patrolled the forts where the villagers were forced to complete Vidion's tasks, or searched for Laik and his friends. Leaving them to fight for their lives against the scarecrows had been Vidion's gravest mistake, and it was a mistake he thought about daily. He needed them dead and thought about the seer's warning; that only his younger brother could put an end to his reign.

As Vidion gazed off into the distance with a look of great displeasure on his face, Sid entered the great hall, which was in terrible shape. The whole castle was now in poor condition, after both time and quarrels had taken a toll on its structure.

The gray and purple clouds still hovered in the sky, which set a mood that only vile men could love.

"Master, may I have a word with you?" asked Sid. Vidion stayed quiet and continued to look off into the distance. Sid approached cautiously and, after a few moments had gone by with no answer, spoke again.

"Forgive me for the intrusion, my Master, but we have discovered how the prisoners have been escaping." Vidion continued to look out of the window, but listened to Sid's findings. For a few months now, prisoners had been disappearing from their camps, and not a single trace had been found. None of the remaining prisoners knew a thing, or at least they pretended not to, which of course, led to an increase in executions. Still, the prisoners kept their lips sealed about the escapes. It was the only hope they had in regards to escaping the dreadful and torturous life that was forced upon them.

"It appears someone has been digging tunnels right beneath the grounds of our forts. We discovered a tunnel that led straight to the washrooms. The prisoners are crawling through their own feces and escaping through the tunnels," Sid informed Vidion. Vidion thought for a moment and turned to Sid. The fear in Sid's face was easy to read, and totally justified, especially since Vidion had been extremely unreasonable as of late. He was frustrated because, although he was finally healed, and his abilities as a sorcerer were at full strength, he still seemed to be a bit short of his ambitions. His brother was still out there, and above all else, it was his very own fault for not killing him when he had the chance.

"Search the rest of the prisons," Vidion demanded. "If they did this to one of our forts, they have done it to others." Sid nodded his head and left toward the dry moat where most of the Aroku tended to gather and wait for orders.

No one could hurt Vidion, or so Vidion thought, but during his trek to spread his evil spells and word, his greed had kicked in once again. Vidion had entered the cave where the ashes were in hope of becoming even stronger. Once he reached the opening where the winds blew warm, he smashed through the rock wall, only to land on the shaft of a torch. The fire from the torch did not hurt him in the slightest, but the shaft left him with a fragment of wood in his arm, which brought great agony. Vidion continued walking toward the remnants of the tomb. The roots and vines had grown throughout the years. As he grabbed them to pull them out of his way, the simple touch of vines burned through his veins, and it was there that he realized he was not as powerful as he thought. *But why?* he wondered. He had a weakness, but the possibility that Laik had robbed him of the ashes of Erthos did not even occur to him. His brother was young and naïve, and he did anything Vidion demanded, including giving him the ashes. Laik had been incapable of betraying him when they were kids, or so he thought, and assumed that that was still the case.

Vidion collapsed from the pain. He woke to find himself outside of the rubble-filled tomb and in the care of Klokus. The creature was the guardian of the ashes, and since Vidion had consumed them, it guarded and protected Vidion as if he were the remains.

It was not the vines and wood that hurt him *per se*. What really hurt him were those *specific* vines and pieces of wood. They were doused in a mixture of rainwater and what remained of the ashes. Years ago, after the cave collapsed, the remains scattered onto the ground and seeped into the soil. In time, storms and heavy rainfall spread the ashes throughout the cavern, and out into a river. The trees and vines that sprouted along the river grew strong with the help of the Gods' remains. Vidion's source of magic rooted only from Airos, Wyolus and Flonius. Since Erthos did not run through Vidion's veins, any tree or piece of nature that grew with Erthos' ashes was a weakness to him. As a result, the wooden shaft of the torch and the vines he pushed away caused him great pain. Not all seeds were peppered with the remains of Erthos. Not all trees grew with such strength, and not all vines sprouted with the ability to harm Vidion.

The tunnels that ran under the forts were man-made, and not a trace of evidence was ever left behind. At the entrances of the tunnels, where there should have been footprints, there were none, and it was the one thing that baffled Sid's mind. In any other case, he would simply have followed the footprints to wherever the prisoners escaped, slaughtered them, and then reported it to his master, but this was different. Not even a cracked twig or crushed leaf was within the vicinity of the tunnels' entrances, and Sid was determined to find out where the escapees had gone.

That night, Sid decided to stay at a tavern that was nearby. It was one of the few taverns that was still open, and only prisoners with special privileges were allowed to enter the bar. The prisoners were branded on their necks, forearms, chests, or shoulders with the symbol of Vidion. Without it, one would be punished and beaten. Ian, Laik, Pike, and Gamet had had themselves branded with Vidion's symbol. It was, of course, done so that they would be able to roam freely throughout the land, and if they were ever caught, their branded bodies served as proof of their freedom.

Sid sat in a corner drinking his ale as he pondered all possibilities. The rest of the men enjoyed their free time and drinks, and laughed at their misfortunes. Their fun, harsh jokes toward one another were the only things that got them through the day, but Sid noticed one thing was off. At the opposite end of the bar, a group of four men sat calmly at a table and paid no mind to the tales and gags the rest of the men shared. It was Laik, Pike, Ian and Gamet, and they had arrived moments after Sid. Since then, they had not behaved the way the rest of the prisoners did. Most prisoners used the time to forget about their troubles, but these four appeared to discuss nothing but their troubles. While the four of them got deep into conversation, Sid slyly slithered into a nearer stool and sat there with his shroud concealing his face. But the men were not stupid. While they did not see his face, they noticed his movement toward them and changed the subject. Shortly after that, the bartender came to their table and handed each of them a round of ale.

"The Aroku rest tonight, but be wary. The prisoners have mentioned that Vidion's men have discovered one of your tunnels. They are on to you. Be careful," said the bartender, then walked away without realizing that Vidion's right-hand man had heard his words. It was then that Sid realized he had found the ones responsible for the missing prisoners, but acting upon it would have been unwise, especially by himself. Sid walked out of the tavern and waited in the woods to follow the men when they emerged from the bar. Hours later, they did, in a drunken stupor as they playfully smacked each other in the face and laughed. They headed deep into the woods, and Sid crept behind them. After what felt like an eternity, the men crossed a swinging bridge hung over a gorge and, at the end of it, turned a corner, after which Sid could not see them any longer. Sid had no choice but to allow them to advance, because one look back while on the bridge would have ended his secrecy.

Once they were out of sight, he quickly, yet quietly, ran across the bridge himself and turned that same corner. The woods and the path continued, but the footprints did not.

Muddled and frustrated, Sid returned to the tavern. By the time he reached the inn, all of the prisoners were back at their forts, and the sun was beginning to rise. The bartender had just finished cleaning and had locked the front door to the tavern. Sid snuck behind him and startled him. The bartender backed up against the locked door, and Sid placed a knife to his throat. The bartender did not fight or resist, for the mere fact that it was Sid, and everyone knew Vidion protected Sid. Everyone knew who Sid was, and everyone feared him. Everywhere he went, people knew to be careful, because anything that occurred around him would end up in Vidion's ear. The only time someone ever tried to oppose Sid, Vidion pulled his limbs apart and forced all of those around to eat his flesh straight from the bone.

"Speak, or I will cut your throat right where you stand. Who were those men? The four men you tipped off?" demanded Sid. The bartender shook in fear and tried to think of something to say without ratting out his friends, but there was nothing he could do or say without losing his life.

"They...They...They were my friends. They mean no harm. Honest!" he answered.

"They mean no harm to you, I'm sure, but I heard what you told them. I was there when you mentioned the tunnels. Now they know we are looking for them. So, not only are they planning to thwart Vidion's plans, but you have betrayed your king as well by helping them," responded Sid. The bartender flinched with Sid's every move and begged for his forgiveness and his life. Sid pushed him to the ground and

136

thought for a moment before answering. "It's okay. We all make mistakes, right?" Sid continued as the bartender nodded his head. "Which is why I will allow you to correct it." The bartender lowered his head in both shame and guilt, because he knew that whatever was going to be asked of him would require him to betray his four friends. However, it was his only chance to avoid certain death and, more than that, it was the best chance he had to protect his wife and children.

"I am certain they will return. Those men come here for your knowledge. Send them to your fort. I want to make sure I am there for their capture, and your fort happens to have more guards than any of the others. Find a way!" Sid requested. "Once they arrive at the fort, I will arrange for their capture. You worry about nothing else, and you will live to see another day. We all make mistakes, but this is your chance to show your loyalty to your king." The bartender agreed with his head and heart, both heavy.

Days went by, and the four men finally walked into the tavern and took their seats. Much like the first time, Sid was unable to see their faces, because they also wore their cloaks over their heads. Sid watched from outside as the bartender acted as naturally as possible. When the bartender served the men their ale, Sid crept next to an open window, where he hid to listen.

"Good evening, gentlemen. Here we have the finest ale you will ever introduce your taste buds to. It is made from the richest and purest of apples that we have. Go on. Give it a try!" said the bartender. The four men gave it a taste, and all of them approved. Apples were a delicacy at this point. After Vidion had cast his spells and spread his foul incantations throughout the lands, even the fruit was not considered safe to eat. Some were healthy, rich in taste, and scrumptious. Others were cursed and

137

came alive, attacking those who came near their tree or decided to pick a fruit from the bunch.

The men continued to enjoy their ale when, finally, one of them asked if there was any word on Vidion and his knowledge of the tunnels.

"There is indeed, my good sirs. Word is, the king, and his hordes of Aroku, are marching south as we speak. They learned of the tunnels you men dug not long ago, and believe you are all in that area. The rest of their forts are still being watched, so be careful. Fort Ogaray is your best bet for your next attempt. That's where I live." The four men took the bartender's words with all of the trust in the world. He was very appreciative of them, because the men had freed his family; his wife and three kids. The bartender was saddened and disappointed at himself for what he had done, and added a few final words to them before they headed out:

"I want to thank you for everything that you have done for us. Please know that, no matter what happens next in your lives and your quests, you are heroes to many. Take care."

The men found it a bit odd, but continued to finish their drinks while they quietly spoke amongst themselves. In the meantime, Sid rode with haste and met with his king, who awaited his return impatiently. He informed Vidion of the situation quickly, and before the sun rose, a dozen of the Aroku and two-dozen archers waited for the men to make their attempt at freeing more of the prisoners.

The tavern was closed by now, and the bartender locked the door as usual before he headed home. Sid returned without warning, and once again stopped him in his tracks.

"You did a great job, and your assistance to King Vidion will not go unnoticed," Sid advised. The bartender was grateful to hear the words, but hated the fact that he had had to betray the four men. "Is there anything I should know?" asked Sid.

"Yes... There is a rumor going around with the men. They say that the one they call Laik has some sort of power, the ability to control soil, trees and vines that are around him. They have a hideout. All of the escapees are there. It's called Leaflake, a forest within the dunes. That's all I have though, I swear." Sid's eyes widened, and he replied.

"Although your assistance to the king is the reason we will soon capture these traitors, Vidion has deemed that you are a traitor as well. He asked me to bring you to him, but a deal is a deal, and I don't like to break mine. I will not be taking you to him. So go. Leave. And I suggest you do not return here."

The bartender did not waste time, and began to run away as fast as he could. Sid drew his bow and an arrow and snickered to himself as he aimed at him. The arrow pierced through the air and straight into the man's back, who let out a grunt. Sid slowly walked to where the bartender struggled to his feet in great pain and pushed him against the closest tree.

"I am a man of my word. I won't take you to Vidion to die, but I never said that I wouldn't take care of you myself." Sid slowly inserted his knife into the man's gut, twisted it, and took it out as the man yelled horribly. He would now bleed out, and there was no stopping it, but his cries annoyed Sid, and he slit his throat to silence him. The dying man's wife watched quietly through a window as she covered the eyes and ears of her children. The tavern was the bartender's and his family's hideout, unbeknownst to Sid who waited and watched the bartender gasp for air.

"My apologies sir, but it had to be done. You know too much," whispered Sid in a sarcastic tone as he watched the bartender die.

Not far from where the tavern lay, the four men slept under the shade of a tree. Their long hair and beards were full of dirt from a bustling night of digging and excavating. The cries of the bartender were so loud that they echoed faintly in the ear of Laik, which woke him up. The rays of the sunrise, which hit his eyes, did not help either. As he stretched, he looked back at his friends who were also getting up, except one of them, Pike.

"We should let him sleep, Laik. He worked hard last night. He must be exhausted," Ian tried to convince his friend. Laik walked toward him with a smile on his face. Pike was entirely out cold, and not even the pebbles Gamet threw at his face were enough to wake him up. Pike was cozy and warm in his blanket, despite the cool breeze, which had had Ian shivering throughout the night.

"We all worked hard, Ian. Plus, if we don't start moving, Vidion and his horde will have a far greater chance of catching us. We finished digging out our tunnel, but we must prepare for tonight. We will free more of the men, women, and children," answered Laik as he stopped right before Pike, unzipped his pants, and flopped out his manhood. The men held their laughter as best as they could, and out came the flow of yellow-golden urine, which splashed upon Pike's face. Within seconds, Pike was awake, and crawled back up against the trunk of the tree as he tried to figure out what had happened. "Who? What? It's so warm!" Pike exclaimed as he continuously spit the urine from his parted lips.

They all laughed at Pike's misfortune, but even he laughed at the fact that his best friend just pissed on his face. It was unheard of, and most friendships would end with such an act, but these were the type of things that oddly brought them closer.

"Let's go. We will head to Leaflake Forest. There we will eat and rest till nightfall. Ogaray is only a day north of there," said Laik. Leaflake was a blessing to men like them, and all of the prisoners they had helped escape. Its location to Vidion and his underlings was unknown, mostly because it was lost in the middle of a plethora of sand dunes that were the size of mountains. The dunes stretched as far as the eye could see, and a hike through them was challenging, to say the least. Those who tried would usually return before they reached the first peak, and their eyes, ears, and mouths would be filled with sand. The prisoners, however, had everything to lose if they were caught. Several hiked over the dunes, and many died after getting lost and becoming dehydrated, but one day some of the prisoners stumbled upon a miracle; Leaflake. It was a vast and very rich forest, which flourished with fruits, vegetables, and plenty of deer to hunt. It had everything the prisoners needed, and they made a home of it. Best of all, not a soul before them knew of the place, and the prisoners worked day and night to pave an easy passage that was known only to them.

Although Ian, Laik, Pike, and Gamet knew of Leaflake, they rarely visited the forest. They spent most of their time finding ways to release more prisoners, and any free time they had was spent in the wilderness or smaller hideouts that were built away from Vidion's kingdom.

As the four of them arrived at Leaflake, the former captives cheered at their presence. They knew them as heroes, and the folks showered them with everything they had to offer. They only accepted what was needed, like food and water. Still, Ian loved the attention and soaked in the attentiveness that his ego so desperately desired.

"Thank you, everyone. Thank you. We are looking for shelter. Tonight we will free more men, women, and children, and if you have the space, we will likely bring them here," said Laik. The townsfolk cheered and yelled out of happiness, and offered to aid them in their quest, but Laik quickly diverted the idea.

"While we do appreciate it and would love the numbers, we stand a much better chance of not getting spotted if we travel in a small group. We've found that the four of us are sufficient enough to get the job done, and it is exactly how we freed all of you." The folks understood and continued to make them feel at home.

As nightfall came, the four of them sat around a fire and reviewed their plan for the night, while they each made sure their weapons were at least in decent condition. Once again, there was no steel or iron. All of the weapons were made of wood, vine, and stone. Their weapons were battered, but weapons were so scarce that even a used and ragged weapon was a good one. One of the villagers noticed the condition of their weapons, and out of gratitude to them for saving his life, he tried to help them.

"Forgive me for listening in, but I couldn't help but notice the poor conditions of your weapons. There is a blacksmith in this very town who is great at what he does. Of course, there is no iron or steel, but he managed to teach himself how to make weapons out of what we have."

"Thank you, sir. We appreciate it, and we will look into it as soon as we return. The weapons we have will suffice for the night," said Ian, in a kind and respectful tone. At the precise moment he finished his sentence, Gamet took a seat on a chair, which practically powdered beneath him. Usually, the men would laugh at him, but they had grown so accustomed to

Gamet breaking things because of his weight that it had become the norm. Pike looked over at the kind villager and asked,

"Do you think the blacksmith is any good at building inde-structible chairs?"

12

The Apple Tree

The dark of night fell upon them by the time the prison camp was in their sight. Gamet and Ian toddled through the tunnel that was only lit by the torches they carried, while Laik and Pike worked their way toward the walls of the fort in secrecy. Four guards stood in plain sight on each tower, which was more than usual. Nonetheless, they thought nothing of it, even though nearly fifty guards were waiting for them within the walls. The prisoners were all locked in their cells, which made things more complicated, since they were usually out of them and working at this time. They were only allowed to sleep for three hours a night.

Gamet and Ian finally reached the inside of the fort through the tunnel and hid behind a small shed where the guards took turns sleeping. Just before they entered the hut from behind, a guard spotted them trying to enter. Gamet quickly grabbed the guard by the foot and pummeled his face into pulp. In the meantime, Ian looked around to see what they were dealing with, and the sight of the fifty guards left him startled, pale, and silent. "What's the matter?" whispered Gamet as he wiped the blood off of his fists and onto his shirt. Ian pointed at the guards, and both of them nearly soiled their pants.

There was no going back at this point. Within a few moments, Laik and Pike would be in the same predicament as they were, and they were not about to abandon their brothers. Ian and Gamet crept as close as they safely could to the guards and waited for the arrival of their friends. They both knew that Pike and Laik were already over the wall and inside, because the guards in the watchtowers were no longer in sight. It meant the guards were either unconscious where they once stood or splattered on the ground on the other side of the wall. As the two of them watched closely, Gamet felt a hand on his shoulder, and without hesitation, turned and punched whoever it was in the face. It was, of course, Pike who received the blow.

"You motherf..." Pike nearly yelled before Laik covered his mouth with his hand.

"I thought you were one of them!" whispered Gamet as he pointed at the guards, who had now noticed that the guards from the towers were missing.

The soldiers split up and searched around the fort in groups of five. Gamet, Laik, Pike, and Ian carefully snuck from point to point, and the head guard's words did not make their task any easier. "Show yourselves! Show yourselves or watch as we burn the prisoners before your very eyes. It is either you or they."

Five of the guards were ordered to look in the back where the cells were, and while Gamet tore open the lock to one of the cells, Laik and Pike swiftly took out the guards. One by one, Ian led the prisoners from that cell to the tunnel and ordered them to wait a few paces into the darkness. Gamet continued to open the cells, and released as many prisoners as possible.

Meanwhile, the guards scavenged through the fort for the four of them.

Gamet had opened all but three of the cells when one of the guards he clobbered finally regained his consciousness. The guard shook off the massive throbbing headache he had and alerted the rest of his colleagues with the sound of his horn. Pike grabbed Gamet by the arm and rushed toward the exit before it was too late. The prisoners that remained in their cells begged for help, and their cries caught the attention of the guards. Laik helped lower the rest of the prisoners into the tunnel, and Pike and Gamet jumped in as soon as the last one was safe. Laik made eye contact with Pike, who knew immediately what was on his mind.

"Go," whispered Laik. "I will distract Vidion's men to ensure you all make it out alive. They haven't discovered this entrance; otherwise, they would already be here. Throw a rope over the north wall. I will make my exit there." Then, with a simple flick of Laik's fingers, a magic spell began to manipulate the soil that formed the burrow. Its viscosity thickened to the point where the pit closed. Pike hated that Laik did not allow him to stay and help, but the safety and responsibility of the prisoners were now on Pike's shoulders. Against his will, Pike led them out to safety and waited for Laik to surface over the north wall.

Laik tried his best to remain unseen and hid behind anything that he could. The guards began to swarm the area group by group, and Laik soon found himself avoiding them in what felt like a maze of cells and walls. Through one outlet, he could hear the remaining prisoners' cries for help. Laik noticed a large number of guards were circling the area. There was nothing he could do, even with his abilities and magic, since he was nowhere near as strong as his brother Vidion. On the other side, more guards were searching, and a few of the Aroku were sniffing for his scent. Laik closed his eyes and paused to think for a moment. He figured to his right was the outlet closest to the cells, and it likely held the highest chance for escape. Laik opened his eyes, and to his left, he could see the shadows of a few men walking toward him. He drew his wooden staff and ran toward the exit on his right, but before he could realize, the guards had doubled in quantity and he had been seen.

The archers began to fire at him, but before he was struck, Laik managed to pick up a wooden slat and used it as a shield. The board soon became useless, though, as it cracked after a few dozen arrows nearly pierced through it, and Laik lobbed it across the faces of a few of the soldiers. His staff proved useful only against four guards, and before long, he found himself running away once again. In his peripheral vision, Laik noticed the rope had just been thrown over the north wall, and made his way to his escape. As he grasped and tugged on the rope, Gamet, Pike, and Ian hoisted him up and over as fast as they could. Laik flicked his fingers once more, and the guards and Aroku, who had bunched up to get him, plunged into a ditch that Laik formed.

The four of them escaped unharmed. Pike, Gamet, Ian, and Laik ran as fast as they could in an attempt to catch up. At the same time, they looked repeatedly behind them for anyone who might have followed. Instead, they witnessed a horror, which they could do nothing about. The prisoners who were left behind in their cells were set ablaze, and the echoes of their cries and shrieks seemed to get louder and louder as they got farther and farther away. Their guilt made them want to return, but they knew that it was already a lost cause. The prisoners were dead, and it was the first time they had failed.

By morning, they all safely reached Leaflake, and those who were wounded and weary were tended to. The rest of them were provided with food and drink, which they had not had in nearly four days.

Laik looked at his staff, which had cracked right in the center. As he tossed his weapon into a fire, he looked at his friends and uttered, "It would be great to have a weapon that would last more than one battle." Pike and Gamet agreed, while Ian sat behind them, flexing and admiring himself. The three of them shook their heads in disbelief before Laik continued to speak.

"When we were kids, I remember a story my grandmother would often tell me. She even shared it with you a time or two, but it always stuck with me, for some reason. The Bloodstone." Pike and Gamet recalled the story with smiles on their faces. Laik spoke of the stone of the gods, which had never been found. No one had bothered to look for it, either, since the villagers of Toewood all believed Elona to be a bit outlandish.

"Yes. Elona had the best stories, no doubt. If only The Bloodstone one were true," Pike exclaimed, which seemed to bother Laik. It was a pet peeve he had had as a boy, that so many people did not believe Elona. Regardless, Laik ignored the comment and continued to speak.

"One day, I am going to face my brother, and I will need much more than a stick to see him fall. I thought that maybe we could put a small hold on our quest to free the prisoners and search for this stone instead. I know you may not believe in its existence, but think about all of the stories my grandmother shared that ended up being true! Look at the ashes, for instance. They were real."

Pike and Gamet looked at one another as if Laik were crazy. They did not agree with his suggestion, and they were not shy to make Laik aware of the fact.

"Listen. We love you, and we are willing to follow you into pits of hell if need be, but don't you feel it would be a bit selfish to leave the other prisoners to die? I know we won't save them all. It's impossible, but the more we wait, the more will die," said Pike. Laik clenched his fist out of frustration and replied.

"Yes, but if we don't find a way to stop Vidion, this will continue until the day we all die. I don't want to live the rest of my life like a prisoner; someone with no home or someone who can roam only because I have the symbol of Vidion branded on my flesh."

"Be that as it may, at least you are free to wander. You may feel *like* a prisoner, but the rest of these people in cages *are* prisoners. You have the chance to live a little. The children behind bars as we speak don't have the slightest clue as to what that feels like. They have no one to call friends or brothers, and some of them don't even know their parents, Laik." Pike stood firm behind his words, and Gamet seemed to agree.

"My grandmother is the reason for hope. She told us what would happen, and I am the only hope to stop Vidion. Why would you not want to find The Bloodstone and put an end to this?" asked Laik, with his voice now raised. Pike hesitated to speak, but the words that came out of his mouth were words that he, Gamet, and Ian all agreed on. Gamet and Ian stood behind him, and passively showed they supported Pike as he voiced the words Laik did not want to hear.

"Laik... Elona is dead, and there is no way to confirm that we even understood correctly. That's for starters. We were kids, Laik, and few of the stories she shared with us have happened. Who's to say that the stories she shared with us were not just stories to ease our minds or keep us entertained? What are the odds that the so-called gods roamed these lands before us? Where is the proof?"

"Faith. That is all the proof we should need," responded Laik. Pike chuckled at the reply and decided to be blunt with his friend and brother about his thoughts on the gods' existence.

"Faith? You expect me to simply *believe* there is something or someone out there watching us while our lives are torn apart? You are asking me to pretend. Let's pretend, and everything will get better! Your faith is based on the stories of an old woman who people believed was loony, and to be quite honest, I'm starting to think you are even more outlandish!" exclaimed Pike.

Laik clenched his fist again and swung at Pike's face. The strike was so hard Pike fell to the ground and was unable to speak or close his jaw. Laik looked at him with regret, but his anger took over, and he stormed off. Ian and Gamet helped their friend up and watched as Laik disappeared into the town.

"Just leave him. Let him relax," suggested Ian.

While Pike regained his composure, one of the prisoners who had just been rescued headed out of Leaflake without a soul noticing. It was odd, because Leaflake was a safe refuge for them, and all of them knew they stood a better chance if they stayed together in large numbers. For one to leave did not make sense, no matter the reason. Nonetheless, the prisoner walked out through the secret passage that ran through the dunes. At the entrance, the fellow began marking the trees to find his way back. After he scratched a few miles' worth of trunks, the man looked behind him to ensure he was still alone before removing the cover that protected his face from the cold. It was Sid.

Sid had disguised himself as a prisoner. He was among those who had been freed at the fort, and watched everything unfold.

He'd witnessed the passageway that vanished, Laik and his capabilities, and all of the released prisoners who were being kept at this hideout. Most importantly, he had discovered the whereabouts of Ian, Pike, Gamet, and Laik, the man who, it was said, was going to be the one to end Vidion and his rule. Sid paced his way back to the great hall, and before long, he found himself on his knee in front of his king. Vidion was frustrated that his time was presumably running short. If he did not get his hands on Laik soon, then the seer's last words would prove true. Laik would soon end his reign.

Pike's father noticed Vidion's frustration and was secretly thrilled that he would soon benefit from his findings. The information he was about to share would surely ease Vidion's mind. Every time he provided Vidion with valuable information or completed a requested task, Sid would be rewarded with more food and riches than he could handle.

"Master, I have news that you will be happy to hear. I bring word of your brother's whereabouts." Vidion nearly froze, because the opportunity to finally end his brother and ensure his reign had finally arrived. Vidion continued to listen impatiently to Sid as he rose from his knee, walked toward a window, and pointed.

"From here, you spend days looking and thinking about your brother, and all along, he has been hiding within the great dunes. All we see is a thousand mounds of sand, but deep within them, there is rich, lush woodland. They call it Leaflake. Your brother Laik and, to my surprise, his friends and my son are there. They have been taking the escapees there in an attempt to start an uprising against you. They are all grown men, my master. I knew that they were, but it caught me by surprise once I saw them. They have changed so much, yet I still recognized them." Sid paused for a moment only to register the amount of time that had gone by before he continued.

"But as I watched and listened to your brother's childish rant about the gods, I realized that he has not grown much inside as a person. He still believes in your grandmother's stories," he said with a chuckle.

Vidion saw this as a weakness on his brother's part. The gods had never been something Vidion believed in. The only things his faith had relied on were sorcery and Ghaldon. He did not believe in the power of the gods or the ashes. In his mind, the ashes were only ingredients that were needed to brew the potion that gave him his strength. Now he only relied on himself, and with his brother finally within his grasp, he thanked Sid before heading down to his chambers where his armor waited for him.

Sid's throat became dry as he walked away, and with a bit of nervousness in his voice, he called to him.

"Master, wait...there is one more thing. I disguised myself as a prisoner when he freed the captives and confirmed something you should know. There was a tunnel where the prisoners escaped, as expected. Still, after the last one jumped into the burrow, the ground began to slither closed. Before I knew it, the hole was completely sealed shut, and it appeared that Laik was responsible for it. I saw him as he made the enchantment, his eyes turning green. The bartender at the tavern confirmed it as well. I think that's what the seer was trying to tell you. I believe he is a sorcerer, my king. Just like you. He can control the power that Erthos once had, and you, on the other hand, are weakened by it."

Vidion punched the pillar he stood next to, breaking a hole right through the stone. It was only then he realized that Laik must have taken the ashes of Erthos from him when they were just kids. As Vidion took the steps that led him down into his chambers, Sid thought about his son once again. He had not seen him in over twenty years, and the last time he was home, he'd murdered Pike's mother in cold blood. It was the worst memory Pike had, and it was one of the only memories that remained about his childhood. It was something he struggled with and a memory that haunted him.

At the moment, Pike's only struggle was the pain in his jaw. He was finally able to open and close it and speak, although he did not wish to share any words. Gamet was hungry as usual, and to his disbelief, he spotted an apple tree filled to the top with fresh fruit. After his failed attempts at knocking a few apples down with a stick, Gamet moved a boulder with his bare hands to help him reach one. The apples were bright red and looked absolutely and perfectly delicious, and his mouth began to water. As he pulled it from its branch, he began to drool a little, and some fell on the apple. At that moment, Gamet heard a grunt of displeasure that sounded way too close for his taste, but after scanning the scene, not a soul was within his sight. Gamet shrugged it off, and as he went for the first mouth-watering bite, the apple opened its eyes and yelled. The apple jumped at his face and bit him with everything it had as Gamet yanked it away and chucked it against the trunk of the tree. The apple splat into a thousand pieces, and the leaves of the tree began to rustle.

Hundreds of living apples jumped to the ground and angrily locked eyes with Gamet.

"You should not have picked an apple from this tree, lad. The tree is cursed, and they do not like to be eaten. Your best bet is to seek the one they call Moki," one of the nearby townsfolk quickly suggested. Gamet felt ridiculous but, just in case, prepared himself for battle.

"Who is Moki?" questioned Gamet.

"He is a green apple. He lives among them, and he is their leader; dumb to the core but soft-hearted and very forgiving."

Gamet wished it was all a lie, but the angry apples that stared at him said otherwise. "And if I can't find this green apple?" he asked, and the villager replied with a smile,

"Then you should probably run."

The flock of apples began to chase him, and for the first time, the roles were reversed, and Gamet was being chased by food. The apples were quick, but every apple that jumped on Gamet ended up as mush. As he ran through the woods, he desperately searched for the green apple they called Moki, but before he knew it, he grew tired and soon found himself cornered. Gamet desperately gasped for air, and just before the apples collectively attacked, the green apple jumped right in front of him and spoke to the army of fruit in a strange language. The apples seemed disappointed, but out of respect for their leader, they returned to their tree and went back to sleep.

Moki jumped onto Gamet and sniffed around as if he smelled something he was familiar with. Once the green apple had finished sniffing, it jumped on to Gamet's shoulder and made itself comfortable. Gamet looked over at it as it tried to fall asleep. Upon returning to Pike and Ian, Gamet explained what had happened and introduced Moki to his friends. It appeared as if Gamet had a soft side to him after all, even though everyone thought of him as solid as a stone. He had a soft spot for living creatures, and this one, since he saved him, had earned a special place in his heart.

"What will you do with him?" asked Pike as he patted the living apple on top of his head.

154

"I don't know... I guess I will keep him around as long as he wants to stay."

13

The Timeworn Scrolls

Laik sat on a fallen tree trunk at the edge of a creek. The only sound was that of the water flowing and the wind rustling through the leaves of the trees. On the surface, he was angry. He was irate at the fact that a friend he considered his brother had implied that Elona was irrational and that her stories were all made up. They loved those stories, and Pike, without doubt, knew how much the stories meant to Laik. But on the inside, he was in agony. He was in pain because he had hurt his best friend and one of the few people left in his life who loved him. Laik had let his anger get the best of him, which had been the case since he reached the age of seventeen. After staring at the water for hours, Laik opened one of the pouches on his belt and pulled out a folded rag. Inside, he safely kept the leaf his grandmother had given him. It was the only thing he had left of Elona after the fire of Toewood burnt everything to the ground. The leaf was, of course, dead by now, but the pattern of its veins was always interesting to him. There were three veins on one side and four on the other, and although it had been years since the leaf was plucked from its place of origin, it still felt like there was some sort of life left in it. What was even stranger was the fact that it did not crumble like an ordinary dead leaf. The leaf had become rigid like a stone.

An older fellow with an old, ragged satchel over his shoulder suddenly appeared and hobbled his way over to Laik as he continued to think about his friends. Upon making eye contact with Laik for a brief moment, the old man smiled, which Laik found odd. Regardless, Laik continued to mind his own business until the old man took a seat right next to him. There was an awkward silence for a few moments while the old man sat there and analyzed Laik without shame. It was as if Laik were an impressive piece of furniture or the world's most beautiful horse.

"May I ask what it is that you are looking for? You have been staring oddly at me for a few moments already," said Laik, who was by now feeling extremely uncomfortable.

"Of course! I'm sorry. My apologies. You just looked familiar, and I believe my suspicions are correct!" Laik turned to him and looked at his face. There was a sort of familiarity to him, but Laik could not clear his memory enough.

"You are Laik. Laik of Toewood. Aren't you?" asked the old man.

"It has been nearly twenty years since I left that place. You look familiar as well, but... wait! Uncle? Uncle Flint?" replied Laik.

"Yes, my boy! I'm happy to see that you remember me! I am old now, so my face has grown a few wrinkles and a beard, but yes! It's me!"

Laik hugged his uncle with sheer excitement. It was a shock to him because, as far as he knew, all of his family was gone.

"I always thought I was alone. I thought you were dead! I'm

so happy to see you!" said Laik.

"Well, my boy, I was fortunate, but when your grandparents passed away, a part of me went with them. I loved them deeply, and I shared the same love and care for your mother and father; your parents. They were all good people." Flint's eyes began to water, and just as Laik took note, he looked away and changed the conversation. It was heartwarming to know that someone besides Laik himself missed them as much as he did.

"Anyway, I stray from my point and purpose," Flint continued. "Your grandmother asked me to take care of you if anything ever happened to her, and it was a promise I took very seriously. The day Toewood was attacked and burnt down, I tried so hard to find you, but you were nowhere to be found. Before I knew it, years went by, and that unwanted and scary feeling you get when you believe someone to be dead began to overcome my thoughts. Little by little, I began to let go, though I still prayed that I would one day find you. And just when I was losing hope, here you are! Elona asked me to give these to you when you were old enough. She made me swear I would never tell anyone, and she wanted them kept a secret, which is why they were always stored away at my home. She wrote these herself. Here, you can keep the satchel as well."

Flint removed the strap of the satchel from around his neck and handed it over to his nephew. Inside were a few ancient and worn-out scrolls. The satchel was now Laik's and as he grabbed one of the scriptures, the hair on the back of his neck rose. In them were unspoken words from his grandmother. It felt as if he was holding a piece of her at this moment in time. Laik hugged the old man and thanked him.

"How did you know it was me?" asked Laik.

"I heard your friends speak your name, and your grandmother told me quite a bit about the future. Some of the things on the scrolls as well, but those are for you to read. I don't know what they all say. When I heard you argue with your friends about The Bloodstone, I knew for certain it was you, and I would like to say one thing. Although they love you and they mean well, The Bloodstone is real. Your grandmother was not crazy, and you will come to see that with the scrolls that are now in your possession." It was a relief for Laik to hear those words, but naturally, he still had his doubts.

"And how are you so sure that it exists? Have you seen it?" asked Laik, full of hope.

"No, actually. I wish I could tell you that I have. I just know because I trusted your grandmother. So I guess you can say I know because I have faith." Laik's hope came crumbling down inside, but he tried his best not to show it. Although he had relied on faith his entire life, he began to feel his friends were indeed right about some things; one of them being his faith. He started to think that there was nothing wrong with faith, but blind faith was another story. Blind faith was to trust without reason, and after the confrontation with Pike, he realized that Pike was mostly right. Laik trusted in what his grandmother said, but believed with no real reason.

"Well, I am delighted to see that you are alive and doing okay, especially to see the good deeds you and your friends are committing. Who knows where we would all be had it not been for you? I know I would have still been held captive or worse. You may not know it, but the people are starting to see you as their leader, Laik."

Laik suddenly felt the weight of the world on his shoulders. He did not wish to be anyone's leader, much less an entire kingdom of people.

"I am no leader, uncle. Believe me. I am no leader. I am weaker than they think... Anyway, I should get back to Leaflake. I need to apologize to my friends, especially Pike." Flint nodded his head in agreement; it was time for Laik to speak to his friends, but he did not agree with one thing.

"Best of luck, Laik. But before you go, I must say this: You motivate people. You have the courage to do what others don't, and you have empathy. I think those are more than enough qualities to say you are a leader. I am proud to follow you, and I know our family would have been as well."

"Thank you," said Laik as he hugged Flint and headed toward the town.

Pike, Ian, and Gamet sat on the stumps of fallen trees. They enjoyed the pleasant foods that they had not been able to eat for some time now, while Moki munched on worms and other insects he found on the ground. As Laik approached, he soon found himself at a loss for words as the four of them acknowledged each other's presence. It was awkward, but one could rest assured that Gamet continued to eat his food. Pike and Ian placed their meal aside before Laik began to search for the words he wanted to share.

"Every time someone has been taken away from me, it made me think about life and how short and fragile it can be. It is hard for me to grasp that from one moment to the next, people could be living in their final moments, and no one knows it until their final breath is taken. It makes me feel as if life does not matter. It feels as if there is no point. What scares me most is that no one knows what happens after we cease to exist. It's hard for me to grasp that, because when the day comes that I die, I do not want to be in darkness. I want to be with my loved ones again. I want there to be an afterlife where the gods walk the same ground that we do, and protect us. The thing I fear most is that when I die, there may be nothing. It would mean that everything I have done, and everything that anyone has accomplished before me, was all for nothing because, eventually, we will all die."

Pike began to feel bad for pushing his beliefs on Laik and realized that his way of thinking was the one thing that gave him internal peace. Still, before he could speak and apologize, Laik stopped him and continued.

"Hold on, please. I'm not done yet, and I need to get this off of my chest. I know that most people do not believe in the gods because there seems to be no proof of their existence, and the little that there is can be explained by mere coincidence or the act of sorcery. Then you have those like myself who believe simply because someone told them so, and it is convenient to believe in the gods. It's basically out of fear. It's easy to believe that you will live again when you die, and you will live among the gods with the loved ones that have gone before you... I'm so sorry, Pike. I did not mean to strike you. It was out of anger and fear, because you were telling me the truth. You were right. I cannot go by blind faith. Not with this. I want there to be something when I die because I am scared. So, when you told me, I hit you because I didn't know what to do with my frustrations. Forgive me."

Pike embraced him with a firm hug and looked at him in the eye.

"You are my brother, Laik, and I forgave you the moment my teeth were filled with dirt. I know your fear got the best of you. No one knows you like I do, but please listen to what I have to say. You don't have to agree with it, but just listen. Although I believe people made up the gods to comfort others with the idea of death, we are all mortal for a reason. We are placed here for a short time to enjoy the things this world has to offer. Unfortunately, some people are driven by greed and want it all for themselves, like Vidion. Immortality would make us greedy beyond what we could imagine. Without death, people would not value life, and this is something that applies whether the gods do or do not exist. So let's move forward from this. Let us grab whatever will and weapons we have and shove them up Vidion's ass."

A massive sigh of relief overcame Laik. He had not thought Pike would forgive him so quickly and easily, but in no time, the four of them were having a few laughs with some ale in hand. Moki rudely introduced himself to Laik as the apple gulped down his ale without asking for permission. Before he knew it, Laik was having a conversation with a drunken apple, which of course, spoke only gibberish to them. Not before long, Flint joined them and reintroduced himself to the men. They remembered him clearly, and enjoyed sharing stories of the past, especially all of the jokes and pranks they used to play on Flint when they were younger. They reminded each other of when Flint had first opened a shop after the safe passage to the market was built. His shop was going great, and all four of them used to swing by daily for his delicious breads. On a day when they did not have enough money, Pike had climbed the roof of Flint's hut and hovered his backside over the edge. When the time came, and Flint stood just beneath him, Pike pushed as much excrement from his colon as possible with one push. Flint was covered in dung, and he stormed off in an irate yet disgusted fashion to bathe and change. The boys had then grabbed what they could and run off before they were seen, and laughed with their bellies full at Flint's misfortune.

The moon was now right above them, and it was time for

them to get their rest. Flint said his farewells, and into his hut he went to sleep for the night. Ian, Pike, Gamet, and Laik walked along together to the cabin that had been designated to Gamet. Once inside, Pike asked a question that had been in his head all night.

"So now that all of this is behind us, what is the plan? What are we going to do to take down your brother, and when will we do it? How should we ready the people? I'm sure they will be more than happy to fight with us! Oh! And the weapons! What will we use to defend ourselves?" asked Pike. Gamet's eyes lit up with glee and excitement as he began to pitch a few ideas that he had up his sleeve, followed by Ian, who also shared a few of his own. Laik watched as they discussed and hated the fact that he was about to tear them apart inside. If there was anything that excited them, it was battle, and all the more when it was against Vidion, who was the root of everything that had gone wrong since they were kids. But before their hopes went higher than they already were, Laik put a halt on their plans and let them know what he had in mind.

"I am going alone," said Laik. "I'm leaving. I know the first thing that is going to come out of all of you is that you are coming with me, but this is something I must do on my own."

"There is no way I am going to leave you to take on Vidion on your own," exclaimed Gamet. "We all know he is much too powerful for any of us alone, but if we stick together, we have a chance. We have a chance while the people in our uprising distract him and take on the Aroku. We can train them and help them understand how to defeat his fiends." But Laik remained conflicted and explained his thoughts.

"My family trusted my uncle Flint with their lives. Sometime in her life, Elona wrote and gave the scrolls in this satchel

163

around my neck to him and trusted him to give them to me when the time was right. The scroll in my hand is about The Bloodstone and... I feel we need this. From what my grandmother explained, it is the one thing that is powerful enough to stop Vidion. I know you may not trust or believe in these sorts of things, which is why I ask that I go alone. I will not and do not feel comfortable with any of you coming with me, and the people of Leaflake need your guidance more than I do. I hope you understand. It is something I feel I have to do."

"We understand," said Pike after a short pause. "We will stay behind and lead the people. Myself, Ian, and Gamet will head to the woods. We will build as many weapons as we can. If you are not back within two days, we hope to meet you in battle." Pike paused for a moment and realized that it could be the last time he saw his friend. He held back his tears in fear of looking weak, and hugged him before bellowing, "You better get back on time, you bastard! We will be waiting! If you don't, I will find your remains and drop a stool on them like you pissed on my face. I promise you." The four of them laughed as Laik packed a few things and said his goodbyes, but before he left, Ian stopped him to share a few words.

"Everything happens when the time is right, my brother. Everything happens when it is meant to happen. For what it's worth, I feel the world is too perfect for there not to be a god. I hope that makes sense to you."

Laik thought about his words for a moment, but "perfect" did not seem to make any sense to him. Laik replied with a smile,

"Perfect? Hmm... I will think about that, Ian. I will sleep on it." Pike and Gamet stood there confused as well, because the world they lived in was far from perfect and perhaps the exact opposite. Laik soon disappeared into the woods, while

Pike felt curious enough to ask, "What the hell do you mean by 'the world is too perfect'? Have you not seen the same things that we have?" Gamet could not care less as he rolled his eyes and headed to his cabin with Moki. Ian explained his thoughts to Pike before the end of the night, and the following morning, the three of them started a day-long quest to make as many weapons as they could out of the gifts of nature. They returned later that evening with a carriage full of them, but it was not nearly enough for every person to wield one. As the men unloaded the weapons into a shack, a villager approached them with a look of confusion.

"If you don't mind me asking, what are you doing?" asked the villager.

"We have spent all day working on these. They are actually for all of us. Weapons! The only weapons we have for when the time comes to take on Vidion and his horde," said Gamet with the utmost confidence. The villager looked at the weapons, and Gamet waited for a compliment on their craft. Instead, the villager asked a question that made them feel like their efforts had been pointless. "Well...why waste all of this time when you could have just asked the blacksmith?"

"The blacksmith?" asked Gamet as his heart sank, and the pain from the blisters on his hands finally caught up with him.

"Yes, the blacksmith right over there. He has hundreds of weapons *already* made, ready for us to wield if need be." Gamet's blood began to boil as he began to realize an entire day of hard labor had practically gone to waste. He informed Pike and Ian, who were also not very thrilled about the news, but rather than throw a fit, they headed to the blacksmith, who was working on a few weapons at the time. The three of them already knew of the blacksmith, but what they didn't know was that the blacksmith had crafted a plethora of weapons already. As they got closer, they could hear and see a few of the villagers making fun of his work and laughing at the blacksmith's expense.

"This guy is a moron! He is making weapons out of wood, which most of us can do on our own!" said a villager.

"Give him a break! He is doing it for the children! These are toys, right?" said another as they continued to laugh and tease. Pike was now inside the shop with Ian and Gamet. The three of them looked around at what the blacksmith had produced. He was a young man, but his work was impeccable, precise, and nearly perfect. The villagers continued with the teasing until Pike finally had enough and confronted them in the nicest way he possibly could.

"Would you guys mind shutting your mouths? It would be most appreciated. I see no point in teasing someone for their work, especially when his work is flawless. I'm willing to bet his feces would look better than anything you have ever built." The villagers suddenly stopped laughing and seemed to ready themselves for a fight, but when they caught sight of the size of Gamet, they quickly eased their attitudes and stopped teasing the blacksmith. Most of the villagers had seen Gamet during their rescue and knew what he was capable of doing when he was angry.

"You men should appreciate the fact that he is willing to provide us with anything at all. You should know that iron and steel is a thing that no longer exists in our world. Why would you make fun of such a situation? In just a few short days, you will be defending yourselves, and all that is good, with these weapons. We should be working together, but it's people like you who ruin things for everyone else," said Pike. The villagers took a few steps back and apologized to the blacksmith. Once the villagers had left, Ian, Pike, and Gamet continued to admire the blacksmith's work.

"Your weapons are amazing. With a skill such as this, surely, you must know how to defend yourself. This is the work of someone who knows everything there is to know about combat. I must ask...why didn't you defend yourself?" asked Pike. The blacksmith stopped what he was doing and attended the gentlemen who had come to his aid.

"Thank you. I appreciate it. I do know a thing or two about defending myself, but I chose to ignore them because they are stupid. Plus, I know that we need all the men we could get. People like that would serve perfectly in the front lines as bait." The four of them laughed together, knowing very well that those in the front lines often did not make it back. Pike continued to ask about the blacksmith's weapons, and it was soon revealed that he had enough for every man at Leaflake, and then some. This was a relief to Ian, Pike, and Gamet, because it meant that they did not have to go through another day of hard labor. Instead, they could begin planning and preparing, which was much needed.

Their laughs and conversations with the blacksmith soon came to an end, and the three of them decided to leave him alone to continue his work. Before they left, however, they each made a purchase. Finally, they held the weapons they were most familiar with since their childhood. They were again very pleased with the quality of their new weapons.

"If you need anything else, feel free to swing by whenever you need to," said the blacksmith. Pike, Ian, and Gamet thanked him for his kindness.

"We will indeed, sir. I don't think we caught your name,

though," said Pike. The blacksmith grabbed his tools, and before he continued to work, he spoke the most unexpected words they thought they would hear.

"My name is Iolas."

14

The Sprout, the Seed, and the Leaf

"I never thought I would live to see the day that my brother would come back into my life. I was just a baby when we were separated, so I don't know much about him. All I know is what uncle Flint shared with me throughout the years. Flint was the only family I had," Iolas said. Pike, Gamet, and Ian listened carefully, still in disbelief. "Uncle Flint told me about everything from my parents to my grandparents, their beliefs, and even about my two brothers. He told me stories about all of you, and all of the mischief you got yourselves into. As terrible as it sounds, I wish I could have been a part of that. When I was younger, I hated my uncle for keeping me a secret. I missed the chance to grow with my brothers. But, as the years went by, I understood. Vidion wanted all of us dead, and I was just an infant. He explained that he'd wanted to take all of you with him as well, but when Toewood fell under attack, none of you were anywhere to be found. He figured when you all saw the damage Toewood had endured, you wouldn't have been stupid enough to show yourselves. I guess he was right, because you are all still here. Anyway, I spent my entire life here in Leaflake.

Most of my life, there were never more than maybe twenty people here, but now we have hundreds. All I really had were a few scrolls my grandmother wanted me to have. Most of them were stories about the family, the gods, and The Bloodstone, which she claimed was real."

Gamet spit out his ale, while Ian's jaw dropped wide open.

"Bloodstone? Did it by any chance have anything to do with the gods?" asked Pike.

"How did you know about it?" Iolas asked, as if he were the only one to know of it.

"Your brother. He has been searching for it since your grandmother first told him. When we were kids, we tried helping him many times, but it always led to a dead end. After all of these years, we have given up, but he never lost faith. He is out there right now looking for it as we speak," said Pike. Iolas thought for a moment, and then it clicked. The scrolls: he had never had a map. They never described where to go or gave a name of a town. He had always been told to look for a tree that stood out among the rest of them.

"His scrolls... did they ever give him a place to search for?" asked Iolas.

"Yes, actually, but it's supposedly hidden on a lost island, and we never found the island," explained Gamet. Iolas' eyes widened as he heard Gamet's words.

"That's because it's not an island he should be looking for. It's a tree, a tree that supposedly doesn't exist anymore. Our grandmother left us with many scrolls, but one of mine had information about the tree. One of his must have the location. She must have done that on purpose; to keep The Bloodstone safe and away from Vidion. I must find him! If you guys have tried helping him before, you must know the general area. I will head in that direction. I'll tell him about everything. I will tell him that I'm alive and tell him about the tree!"

Pike accompanied Iolas on his quest to meet with his brother, while Ian and Gamet stayed behind to help prepare. On the way, Pike and Iolas shared stories of their youth and the crazy things they did to survive.

In the meantime, Laik once again found himself where the map always took him. The search for The Bloodstone had proven pointless time and time again, but it was the first time in a while that he had had a silent moment to himself. Laik pulled out the scroll his uncle Flint had advised him to read and began reading:

"If you are reading this, Vidion is in control now, and most of the people you knew as a child are no longer with you. I wish I could tell you that I had more to say to you about the future, but this is as far as the seer's eye allowed me to see. All of the things I kept from you were for a reason. I hope you understand that it was not to make things difficult for you. It was to make things difficult for Vidion. Keeping the future from you was a way to ensure the course of the future did not change. The eye revealed what was to come if I told you of the coming days. You would have done everything in your power to change the misfortunes of your loved ones, but in doing so, Vidion would have succeeded. It would have caused a trickle of events in his favor. The path you are on now is the best chance there is, but there is no surety.

Even though I cannot tell you of what is to come, I can tell you about The Bloodstone. Temptation is a powerful thing, Laik, especially when your loved ones are at stake. For that reason, I must admit that I lied, Laik. I lied to you about The Bloodstone. Although it does exist, there is a missing piece to the puzzle, and that is why you have not been able to find it all of these years. The Bloodstone is within a cave on the lost island, and the map that will guide you there is on this very scroll. All you have to do is wet this old scroll, and it will reveal itself. You will also need the half of the leaf I gave you when I died, but it will be useless unless you get your hands on the other half. This leaf is the key to The Bloodstone, but your brother has the other half. You must get a hold of it.

I have no doubt about you accomplishing what you set out to do. You carry the blood of your father, Laik, and at times I wish I would have told you when I was alive, but your father carries the blood of the gods. Only those who have this blood in their veins can bring The Bloodstone forth. The gods are watching over you, Laik. They are on your side. The Bloodstone is the only way to see the demise of Vidion. May it fall kindly in your hands and protect you from everything that is to come.

Your Grandmother,

Elona

Laik rolled the scroll back up, and into his satchel it went. *How am I going to get the leaf from Vidion?* he thought to himself. He was not upset at the secrecy, but he was frustrated. All of his efforts in the past had been for nothing, but the safety of The Bloodstone was important and he understood. Before he knew it, Pike strolled up, with a young man he had never seen before. He had dirty blonde hair and the same color of eyes Laik did.

"Pike! What are you doing here? And who have you brought along?" Pike smiled at the news he was about to share and placed his hand on Laik's shoulder.

"You have considered us and called us brothers for many years now, and this will be difficult to believe and take in, Laik. We were at the blacksmith's shop—this is the blacksmith—when we learned his name. We later spoke some more, and he mentioned where he was born. He spoke to us about his upbringing," said Pike. Iolas stood by and waited for him to break the news to his older brother. He had never laid eyes upon him before but, since the moment he had, he had begun to see the similarities in appearance. "This man right here is from Toewood," Pike continued.

"Oh! It's great to meet you. Most of the people who once lived there are very old or no longer with us. How did you manage to survive?" asked Laik, clueless to the fact that he was speaking to his long-lost brother.

"He was only a baby when his cabin was set ablaze and Flint saved him," Pike interjected.

"Flint? He is my uncle. He is a great man," Laik said to Iolas, as he looked over at Pike before gathering his belongings. "I appreciate you sharing the news with me, Pike, but I must continue what I set out to do." Pike smirked and urged Iolas to spit the news out. Iolas was nervous but, after taking a deep breath, he advised his brother of his name.

"My name is Iolas, Laik. I am your brother."

Laik looked back and forth between him and Pike for a few seconds and, after realizing it was not a joke, he embraced his little brother as tight as he could. Both of them had thought the other was dead, and they expressed how happy they were to learn otherwise. Iolas briefly explained how Flint had looked after him, and told him all about what he knew of Elona and the rest of their family. It was nothing that Laik hadn't heard before, but he enjoyed the reminiscing. The men immediately started a fire for some warmth and food, while they caught up and shared stories with each other. It was the first time in a long time that Laik forgot about all of his troubles, and the first time ever that Iolas felt like he belonged. After their meal, and story after story, Pike and the two brothers strayed into a conversation about their older brother, Vidion. Laik's anxiety began to return at the thought of him, and before the stars began to shine, he explained what he had just read in Elona's letter.

Iolas reached into one of the pockets that ran across his chest strap and pulled out a folded piece of cloth.

"Here. This must belong to you, then," said Iolas as he handed it to him. Laik unfolded the flaps and, to his surprise, revealed the second half of the leaf.

"Just when I thought I couldn't be happier to have you back in my life, you decide to present me with this!" exclaimed Laik as he hugged his little brother. Naturally, Laik did not stop to think that the brother who held the other half was Iolas and not Vidion. This was, of course, because he had thought he was dead. With both parts now in his possession, Laik packed up his belongings and excused himself. The men noted his urgency, and before he gave his farewells he made a suggestion.

"Pike, you should go back and help the others. They need all the help they can get. Try to get as many of the women, children, and elderly out. The rest of them will have to be ready for whatever comes." Pike agreed, but before leaving, he made a suggestion himself.

"It would be a great time to catch up with your brother. Why don't you let him come along? Plus, you could possibly use the help," said Pike. Laik agreed, and they soon found themselves soaking the scroll and hiking toward their destination.

Iolas and Laik walked next to each other and continued sharing stories. The conversation helped the time pass quickly, because in the midst of urgency and in the midst of their anxieties, they learned things about themselves and about their family that the other did not know. Eventually, the night fell upon them and their eyes began to feel heavy. In an effort to stay awake, Iolas began to collect and toss a few pebbles, and continued to speak to his brother.

"So! Pike told me about everything you have done for them throughout the years. I don't remember our grandmother, but everything Pike explained and the stories our uncle Flint shared with me leads me to believe she would have been very proud of you." Laik agreed, but his drowsiness left him with few words.

"Thank you... So what is your story? What have you been up to all of this time?" asked Laik.

"Plenty, actually. Most of my life, however, was spent in training with Flint. He taught me everything I know. He taught me how to read, write, and fight, and he taught me the skills of a blacksmith. Once I learned how to make weapons, that was it. My life's purpose was to make weapons, or so I thought, but when I was old enough, Flint began to share things with me that I had never thought imaginable." Laik's interest was at first poor at best but the mere mention of their uncle and secrets began to wake him up.

"He told me about Elona and the eye that she once held. The Bloodstone you are looking for... None of us even knew what it looked like, but Elona made sure to keep it away from Vidion. Neither of us would have been able to find it unless we met." Laik's attention was now fully engaged, and he asked Iolas what he meant.

"When I was about eight years of age, uncle Flint told me about the stories of the haunted forest, and how the shadow that haunted it had not been seen since I was an infant. Naturally, I was always scared, but once he taught me how to make spears

175

and swords and axes, I wanted to make my own weapons. I needed the wood that the forest provided. Uncle Flint was the one who forced me to walk into the haunted woodlands, and although I was frightened to the bone, I was determined to build my own arsenal of weapons. It was never really a desire I had *per se*. I actually pursued it because of a dream I had of an old woman, who told me that the wood from the far west end of the forest was unlike the wood from the everyday trees. It was grown from the waters of Deity Falls. In my dreams, the old woman explained that the ashes of the gods were dropped into the shallow waters, where they were enshrined. When the remains met with the water, they seeped in to Deity Lake, which flowed over a cliff on the very top of the mountain. It was the source of the waterfall, and when the water met with the land at the bottom of the fall, the enchanted waters soaked into the soil. After a few years, the water eventually met with seed. Everything the water touched grew at a rapid rate, but these trees were contained along the edge of the river. Eventually, the weathering did away with this mystical source of water and the trees remained there until uncle Flint spoke to me of Elona for the first time. He handed me a letter she left for me; a scroll. On it, she explained that the trees could be used for much more than the average tree. Their strength was much greater than that of a steel blade, even; at least against Vidion's curses. So I began to make spears, hammers, bows and arrows, and even swords. They were effective beyond what I could ever have imagined, which I learned when I took out one of the Aroku on my own. When pierced by my weapons, the creatures melted on the spot and left behind nothing but a pile of obsidian. I tried to explain it to the villagers, but they all thought I was crazy. I became the town loon and everyone made fun of me for it."

Laik continued to listen carefully as he recalled the times when his grandmother was known as a crazy old lady. He began to sympathize with his younger brother, who had apparently suffered the same fate. Elona had hated the fact that no one believed her, and it hurt her terribly, since she was only trying to care for the people she loved. Regardless, Laik kept his mouth shut and allowed Iolas to finish.

"In Elona's letter, she explained she had split our leaf in two. She did this to make sure Vidion did not get his hands on it. On this island that we are headed to, there is an engraving, and it matches the same shape and size of the two halves. Place them on there. That will open the doors to where The Bloodstone is being kept." Laik was thankful for the information, and the both of them began to pick up the pace.

As Pike made his journey back to Leaflake, he began to notice engravings himself. On the trees nearest to the dunes, Pike caught sight of the scratches that had been left behind by Sid. They were rather odd, and instead of heading back to Leaflake, he decided to follow the trail to learn about the end point. After a long hike, the trail led him to the tavern, where all of the privileged prisoners would usually be at this hour, drinking, laughing and having a good time. But the tavern was empty, like a ghost town, and what made it even more eerie was the fact that the front door had been left slightly open. At the foot of the door, Pike spotted a trail of blood, which led inside.

With a hatchet drawn, he entered carefully and scoped the place out. The blood led behind the bar and there was the bartender's lifeless body, which was being held by his wife. Pike quickly checked to see if there was something he could do, but before long, he looked into the widow's eyes; she knew her husband was already gone.

177

"Who did this?" asked Pike. The widow tried to calm herself down to speak and explained what had happened.

"It...It was one of Vidion's men. I couldn't hear exactly what was said because I was in the other room when my husband was trying to get in but... my husband was only trying to protect me. He was trying to protect his kids. The man told him he would kill us if he didn't tell him. He had to." Pike's concerns grew greatly and he tried his best to quickly calm her and understand what she spoke of.

"Okay. It's okay. You and your kids are safe. But please. Tell me. Help me keep the others safe. What did this man want? Where was he headed? What did your husband tell him?" asked Pike, and when she found the courage to admit what his husband had done, her tears began to fall like rain from a heavy cloud.

"Leaflake! He wanted to know where the prisoners had gone! My husband was only trying to protect his family. Please don't be mad at him!" she cried. Pike grabbed his hatchet and raced toward the town. He immediately knew Vidion's men must be marching toward Leaflake and not a soul in the town was aware of it. By the time he arrived, his fears proved to be true. The town was under attack, and the Aroku were demolishing the village. Iolas' weapons were not dispersed amongst the villagers before the ambush. With only standard sticks and stones to defend themselves, the fiends gradually destroyed their homes, their food and their people. Pike caught a glimpse of Gamet who fought off as many Aroku as he could. The people whose lives he saved all headed to the top of the dunes, where the Aroku would not climb for fear of drying out like a mug of water spilled into the sand. Pike did what he could to do the same, and as the last of the villagers climbed up the dunes,

Pike looked back to see a child in danger. He was pierced in the chest and unable to defend himself. A barrel of ale was the closest thing to Pike, which he lit on fire and rolled away to grab the attention of the two Aroku who were attacking the boy. They began to march toward Pike, and in the meantime, Gamet came and scooped the child off the ground and safely onto the dunes. Almost the entire town had been destroyed, and just as they thought things could not get worse, the man who was responsible for all of this havoc turned the corner and walked toward the foot of the dunes. Vidion watched the child's skin turn pale, and the rest of the survivors trembled in fear.

"Where is my brother? Where is Laik?" growled Vidion. Gamet placed the child on the ground and took a few steps toward the king, only to spit in his presence. Vidion chuckled at the act and soon recognized who he was.

"You. You are his friend; the fat one. The child... the one who is about to die...is he one of your sons? Or do you always care for people who do not matter?" asked Vidion, only to further anger Gamet. The king looked over at the child, who was trembling, and without an ounce of remorse, he asked, "How does it feel, boy? How does it feel to know that, in a few moments, you will no longer exist? Everything you have done with your short pathetic life will no longer matter and soon there will be nothing but darkness."

"Shut your crusty face!" yelled Gamet, who was ready to fight despite the fact that he knew he would not succeed. Ian calmed Gamet down as best as he could before trying to speak to Vidion, while Pike tried his best to save the boy. He knew that it would be difficult to reason with him and took a different route.

"I know the only way any of us are getting out of this alive is if you want us to; if you let us. I am asking you, please; tell me what it is that you want and I will do what I can to give it to you. Let these people live. Their escape and treason toward you is not their fault. It is mine. I freed them, and I let them stay."

Vidion listened and remained silent for a moment. What he wanted was his brother dead, but after years of being unable to find him, he figured the best thing would be to get him to come to him. From a distance, Ian began to feel Vidion's grip around his throat, and the king lifted him and tossed him before his very own feet. Ian looked up and into his eyes, prepared for the worst, but instead of ending his life, Vidion shared a few words.

"Weren't you the one who believed everything Elona fed you? Just like my weak brother?" Vidion bound his feet and his arms together and tossed him into the arms of his Aroku, which took him away. Pike grabbed Gamet by the arm who appeared ready to leap forward at him.

"It's a trap, Gamet. He isn't going to kill him. He's bait," whispered Pike. Gamet tried his best to keep his cool and lowered his weapon.

"Bring him to me. Bring my brother to me, or your friend dies. You have until the next nightfall," said Vidion as he and his horde vanished with Ian.

The smoke from the burned homes rose up into the air and formed a large black and gray cloud. Despite the fact that Laik and Iolas were far from Leaflake, the surge of smoke in the air caught their attention, and was indeed unnatural. The both of them agreed to have Iolas return and help, while Laik continued on his quest for The Bloodstone. The location of the lost island appeared to be in the largest lake Laik had ever come across. It was filled with fog, which made it difficult to see, and on the surface of the lake he witnessed the strangest fish and creatures he had ever laid eyes on. It was terrifying, but once he paddled into the middle of the lake, he began to look around and analyze his map. There was no indication of an actual island, but as he stayed afloat in the same spot for some time, the water began to part and an island began to surface. It was the lost island, and in the distance he could see the cave.

As Laik reached the entrance, he realized that he would have never found it without the map. Roots, rocks, and vines, which created a sort of maze, largely covered it. It was old and cold, and the stone walls creaked and cracked. At the end of the cave, a large room mesmerized Laik, and in the center, a pedestal with an inscription waited for him. It seemed to have partially eroded after the years upon years that it remained hidden, untouched, and underwater. Above it, an engraving, which resembled the two parts of his leaf, stared back at him. Laik placed them into the engraving before him and after a few moments, a dead tree that was just a few paces away slowly began to flourish with life. Like an enchantment, it began to dwindle down into the shape of an imperfect sword, and it was as if the entire tree had somehow squeezed itself into it. It was only then that the faded engravings began to make sense to him. The Bloodstone was not a stone at all; it was a sword.

The sword was, of course, made of the same wood, leaf, and vines from the tree, but Laik knew it had to be special. Despite the fact that it was taking shape before his very eyes, Laik felt the presence of an unknown power as he got closer to the sword. It almost felt as if it were pulling him closer, and the tension in his chest increased with every step he took. His body became weak, but just before he fainted, he grabbed the hilt of the sword. From the hilt and blade, the wood, leaves, and vines began to wrap around his arm, ensuring that the sword would not leave his grasp. The vines and wood continued to crawl up his arm and around his body, creating a sort of armor. It protected him better than any armor he had ever put on, and provided a sheath for the sword as well. Laik now had the spirit of the gods in his hands, and the power of their protection, and with that in mind, he whispered to the gods.

"If you are indeed real, and this isn't just sorcery or magic, please help me. Help us. Give me the guidance I need to put an end to this and save us from Vidion. Let us be rid of this evil and restore the lives we once had. Help me bring back a peace of mind and meaning to life."

By then, Iolas had arrived at Leaflake, only to discover the havoc that was left behind. The remaining survivors had returned from the dunes and tried to salvage what they could. Most of the weapons had burnt to a crisp, including a good number of Iolas', but that was the least of his concerns as his eyes met with the boy who was now in his final moments. Iolas ran to where he was and grabbed his hand so that he would not feel alone. Pike held his other hand, while Gamet tried his best to make the boy feel comfortable. As the boy opened his eyes, the sight of Iolas made him smile, for Iolas was one of the few people in the village who not only acknowledged him but had also befriended him and cared for him. Then, as the feeling of death arrived and his breaths became shorter, the boy began to cry, "I want my mommy. I want my mommy," as he closed his eyes for the final time.

15

Gronlin

The rest of the faded scripture was a stark warning to whoever pulled the sword from its depths. Still, it was impossible to read, which pushed Laik to ignore it. After sheathing the sword behind his back, the vines and wood that armored him withdrew back into the hilt and blade. Before he left, he took a glance around the cave and picked up the two parts of the leaf. As he walked out of the room where the tree and sword sprouted, the ground beneath him began to shake violently. Laik ran as fast as he could, realizing that the grounds were giving way and splitting apart. It was as if the gods were angry with him and were ripping the ground open with their bare hands. All around him, the walls began to cave in, and blocked the exit. An opening that formed above him seemed to be the only way out. As he climbed out of it, the cool breeze hit his face. He could see the rocks and dirt and bushes began to gather as one, and before Laik could run off and escape to his boat, he found himself higher and higher on what must have been a mountain.

Laik struggled to get to his feet, the shaking stopped for a few moments, and he could see everything from where he stood.

It was the highest point he'd ever stood upon, and the thin air did not make anything easier. It was cold, freezing, and it was difficult to breathe because of the altitude. Laik looked into the distance and witnessed the dense smoke that rose from Leaflake. He immediately thought he must return, but before he could take a single step downhill, a deep growl shook the grounds. Upon looking up, he realized he was on the shoulder of a titan, and this titan was the size of the largest mountain he had ever seen. His name was Gronlin, as described by Elona in one of her stories.

The titan was now slowly heading toward Leaflake. Although Pike, Gamet, and the rest of the villagers could feel every step Gronlin took, they were unable to see the giant because of the dunes that surrounded them. Despite the tremors, the townsfolk began to gather whatever was left and whatever was still useful. Most of the shelters were destroyed, and weapons crushed. Bodies of the dead were still spread throughout the town, and their primary concern became burying them with respect.

In the meantime, Laik made his way to the titan's head, where Gronlin's eyes watched and observed anything that moved. The smoke in the air was like a signal for the titan and he walked toward it. Near the very top, Laik could see the pedestal where the engravings and markings called out to him.

Every step Gronlin took shattered parts of the ground and walls near Laik, which made things difficult. Routes would change, and what once appeared to be an easy path to the peak of the mountain would become a perilous and unforgiving slope. As if that were not dangerous enough, the rocks and boulders being shed from Gronlin's body came tumbling down, nearly crushing Laik with every step Gronlin took. Laik took cover behind a boulder that settled, using the time wisely to catch his breath. To the right of him, he could see the smoke from Leaflake, and he pictured the hundreds of freed prisoners in turmoil. In the opposite direction, he could see Vidion and his horde of Aroku, which were made of volcanic rock, at the front gates of his kingdom. Below him was a steep drop, and on the sides that appeared easier to climb down, the journey to the bottom would still take hours to make. Regardless, leaving was not an option. Gronlin was nearly halfway to Leaflake with his slow yet large and long steps.

Laik looked up at the sky, which was dark and gray. He could see that the sun was still up, but the clouds and darkness from Vidion's curse made it difficult to see the light. There was no sign of any hope, no matter which direction Laik looked in. His mind began to race, which he hated, especially at a time like this. *How could this be?* he thought to himself.

I have spent my entire life believing in the gods, believing every word my grandmother told me. But the gods... where are they? Where are they now? Where are they when you need them the most? I am expected to just believe? Blind faith? I am tired of spending my nights thinking with tears in my eyes, waiting, and hoping, and praying that the gods will save us. Pike and Gamet were right. It's all just for comfort; the idea that they are out there watching over us. The idea that we are not alone in our struggles... but we are. The gods were probably just another story created to take advantage of people. They were lies to create a world where those who sin would be punished and those who do not would be saved and protected... Laik stood up yet again with tears in his eyes and shouted toward the skies. "I have not sinned! I have only done what was necessary to protect your people! Where are you now? Where are you now?!" he shouted at the gods.

He raced to the top of the peak with nothing but rage in his blood, and before he knew it, despite the struggles and dangerous conditions, he was at the top. Gronlin was now very close to the village, and cast a dark shadow over Leaflake. Pike and Gamet looked up, and for the first time in their lives, they feared what was ahead of them. Moki ran toward his home and warned as many of the apples as he could. The apples all ran for safety; Moki running back on to Gamet's shoulder.

Similarly, Pike scrambled to get as many people out as he could, but not everyone was in the same condition. Many of the villagers were old and could only move so fast. Another large number of them had been hurt and left to die by Vidion. Pike knew very well that this new monster was much too big for any number of them, and that getting everyone out alive would not be possible.

"Gamet! Go! Take all of the weak and wounded to a safe place. I will meet you there!" commanded Pike.

Gamet looked over at him as if he were crazy and asked, "What are you doing, Pike? We cannot save them. We cannot save them all! You must come. You do not stand a chance against a living mountain. It will crush you!"

Pike agreed with his statement, but he could not live with himself if he did not try. As Pike ran toward Gronlin, Gamet decided he would go and help him, but before he could take two steps forward, an elderly couple happened to stop him and ask for his help. Although every bone in his body wished to help his friend and brother, the couple stood there, helpless. Gamet hesitated but picked them up, threw them over his shoulders, and raced toward safer ground.

On top of the peak, Laik finally reached the ruins of the cave. It was unrecognizable, but at the end of what was once an enormous cavern, the engraved pedestal gleamed brightly. It was the only thing that was still intact and appeared to be part of the titan Gronlin. Laik walked toward the stand to take a closer look. The fact that it was glowing was rather odd to him and he figured it must have had something to do with Gronlin, and the reason the mountain was alive. But just before things appeared too simple, a few of the Aroku rose like the dead from their graves. Laik was well aware of their strength, once witnessing one of the fiends successfully take on more than four men. At this point, the gods were no more in his mind, and before showing himself to the horde, he closed his eyes and took a deep breath.

Upon drawing the sword of the gods, he was once again fully armored by the vines and wood from the hilt. Laik ran toward the nearest monster, and although it managed to strike Laik a few times, the power of the sword was more than enough to slice through the obsidian as if it were flesh. It was astonishing because the few times Laik had encountered one of these, it had taken more than five men to defeat one, and the effort was relentless. It was like chopping through wood with a dull blade. Regardless, now the fiend fell and crumbled to the ground, and the attention of the remaining Aroku was now on Laik. The Aroku surrounded him, leaving him with no option other than to fight. Laik cast a spell on the ground beneath them, which gave way, and the Aroku fell into the pits, which ended their threat. Just a few paces away, the pedestal awaited Laik.

Gronlin was now at the foot of the dunes. The mountain stepped on the dune closest to the edge and flattened it. At this point, Pike was at the top of the dune nearest to Leaflake, and upon gazing at the full size of Gronlin, Pike realized that stopping it was out of the question. Pike slid down the dunes on his shield, indubitably eating a mouth full of sand at the very end. Gamet had taken a good number of the elderly folks out of harm's way by this time, but there were still plenty of villagers who were in need of help.

The soil and rock that rested before the glowing pedestal suddenly gave way just before Laik could reach it. The Aroku were not dead, and the threat was not over. They were made of rock, and a pit was not enough to stop them. Like mice underground, they burrowed their way to the platform as if they were protecting it. The Aroku attacked Laik at once, bashing and thrashing him from one side of the room to the other. At best, Laik became bruised and battered, but the armor proved to be too strong for Vidion's army and their weapons. Their weapons were mostly stone, but they were sharpened to the point where they resembled the past weapons of steel. Laik's armor was practically impenetrable, but the thrashing was becoming a bit much for him, even with the power and the sword he possessed. Regardless, swing after swing, the Aroku began to drop. Even though he was outnumbered and it took him a long while to regain control, the fiends fell one by one, succumbing to The Bloodstone.

As Gronlin took another step, the mountain shook violently. Laik stepped up to the platform when the trembling subdued, carefully looking at the glow of the engraving. Down the center of the leaf, a slit was left open where the stem would usually be. As he desperately gasped to catch his breath in the thin, cold air, Laik raised his sword with the blade facing down and implanted it into the slit in the stone. After a moment, Gronlin began to snarl in pain, and parts of the mountain around him began to collapse. Laik pulled the sword out, and rushed outside, where he was met with a treacherously steep path to the bottom of the mountain. Boulder after boulder came rolling down, often knocking Laik to the ground. If it were not for the armor, he would have suffered a painful death, but the protection kept him alive, and the will to protect his loved ones kept him from stopping.

Gronlin slowly came to a halt, its knees began to collapse, and its body settled on the ground. The mountain had destroyed everything in its path, but at the same time, the impressions his steps made created a plethora of lakes, valleys, and soon-to-be forests. Gronlin's threat was now no more, and its body became a mountain; Mt. Gronlin, to be exact. It was now the most massive mountain to ever exist, and it stretched from Leaflake to what was once known to many as Toewood.

The sands that created the dunes were lifted into the air, and formed an odd color in the sky. It was an orange-reddish color, and the abundant trees of Leaflake protected the survivors from it for the most part. Pike and Gamet caught their breaths while they expected and waited for the worst to arise. They were unsure what to expect since Gronlin had suddenly stopped. Iolas had finally arrived after rushing back to Leaflake, and Pike and Gamet were relieved to see him. After some time, Laik reached the bottom. Pike and Gamet watched as a figure emerged from the clouded, sand-filled air that obscured their vision. Their weapons were drawn in preparation to fight, but when the figure became clearer, Iolas recognized the sword and armor. He had seen it before on many of Elona's scrolls. "It's Laik. He found The Bloodstone," Iolas shouted. Laik placed his sword in his sheath and, before everyone, revealed his face. The people cheered his return after learning he was the one who stopped Gronlin.

Pike, Gamet, Laik, and Iolas gathered inside one of the few

remaining cabins and tried their best to tend to Laik's wounds. He was severely bruised and faint, but it was not enough to stop him from what had had to be done.

"Where is Ian?" he asked. Iolas looked over at Gamet and Pike, who were saddened by the question. They knew it would not sit well with Laik.

"Vidion was here, Laik. When I made my way back to Leaflake after leaving you, I noticed there were odd markings on the trees that led to the tavern. I followed them, and the bartender was dead when I got there, but his wife told me what happened. There was a man who threatened him with the lives of his kids. The bartender spoke to protect his kids and gave him the information on our whereabouts. This man is the right-hand man of Vidion and helped him find us. His Aroku ambushed us just before this mountain began walking toward us... and Vidion came with them. He took Ian... He said that you had until tomorrow night to face him if you ever wanted to see him alive again," Pike informed his friend.

Laik was at a loss for words. He was irate, but tried his best to control himself. He thought to himself that the gods had once again failed not only him, but his friends as well. Pike noticed the look of defeat in his face and placed his hand on Laik's shoulder. He knew that Laik was distraught after witnessing all of the death and the loss of yet another friend.

"He mentioned you before he was taken; before we were ambushed. He wanted you to know why the world was too perfect. He said he found it peculiar that trees give us life. They provide the fruit that we eat, the shelter that protects us from the wild, and the wood we burn for the warmth we need on cold nights like this one. The skies; they give us the water that is needed by all life. Death is only a part of life, but it does not mean that it is a bad thing. Life is all about balance, and if there were no such thing as the gods, we wouldn't have such a perfect balance. He mentioned that if his life ended before old age, then it was simply his turn to rest."

Laik's eyes watered. Ian was the one person who never gave up faith in the gods, no matter how bad things got. In turn, Laik now found it impossible to believe, but the words Ian left behind for him made him think, *Is our world perfect? Despite all that is evil... is it possible?* Laik sat there for a few moments while his friends let him be. They waited just outside of the cabin, which sat next to Iolas' shop. Half the weapons were burnt to a crisp, but those that were left were given to the townsfolk who were willing to fight. As the last of the weapons were passed out, Iolas turned to Pike and Gamet.

"I have weapons for us as well."

"There is no need for them. I am fine with mine. Not as strong as steel, but the same applies to all of us," said Gamet; Moki agreeing with his every word while he filled his mouth with worms.

"No, no. These are different. I hiked along the Deity River, and in the upper streams of Deity Falls, where the river was born, I found a sapling that I had never seen before. It was not from around here, and as I got closer for a better look, I could feel the massive roots beneath it. It was strange to find one with roots that large, so I took as much of the roots as I could, thinking it could be of some use. I was only able to take a few loose chunks. The rest of it was imbedded into the ground and impossible to remove. Once I loaded the few pieces on my horse, the ground swallowed the rest whole, quickly filling itself with deep, freezing waters. It took me up until a few nights ago to finish, but I eventually forged weapons out of them. Like I said, the roots were unlike any other and were difficult to cut and shape. They were strong, very strong. It took me four times the amount of time it used to take me to forge with steel, but I managed to shape them into weapons for each of us." Iolas left for his shop to get the weapons he spoke of, and after a short while, Laik finally surfaced from the cabin.

Pike noticed the look of sorrow in his face. He appeared to be defeated inside; his faith no longer present.

"Your sword. Where is it?" asked Pike, concerned that he had given up. Pike marched inside of the cabin to fetch it for him. The sword leaned against a wall, and upon Pike's grasping of the hilt, the whole thing disintegrated. Pike's heart sank, but as he took a few steps back to tell Laik what had happened, the sword took its form once again. Pike was dumbfounded, but after trying to grab it again with the same results, he realized that only Laik was likely able to wield the sword. Laik walked inside and laughed at Pike, who was utterly staggered.

"It is supposedly only for those who share the blood of the gods. I think it is a curse. I believe it only responds to me because I unearthed it," said Laik.

Pike looked up at his friend, happy to see that he had recollected his thoughts.

"What will we do now? What will you have us do?" asked Pike. Laik took a deep breath and placed his hand upon Pike's shoulder. The look on Laik's face spoke sorrow and despair, but in the gleam of his eyes, Pike could see determination. He could see that Laik had not given up on his friends, and the people who needed him most.

"There is only so much praying a man can do," said Laik.

Outside of the cabin, the villagers were all preparing for combat while they awaited word from Laik. Iolas returned with the weapons he had made and handed a pair of hatchets and a bow and arrow to Pike, who was most grateful. For Gamet, he presented him with a double-sided weapon. On one side was a blunt and sturdy mallet, and on the other was an ax. For himself, Iolas kept a sword. At the center of Leaflake, where all of the villagers gathered, Laik jumped on top of a rock so that he could see everyone, and everyone could see him. The townsfolk slowly stopped what they were doing and lent an ear in the direction of Laik.

"I wish I could stand here before you and tell you that you have nothing to fear. Not far from here, not only lie the fields where our fates will be decided, but there also lies the final resting ground for many of us. The truth is that we are weak, and we are weary. We have little food to regain our strength and lesser numbers to go against a legion that is fiercer than any army our world has ever seen... but our spirits are strong... and they cannot take that from us. Not like the blades we once used to protect ourselves. Not like our loved ones who are here no more. Not like the faith that we hold on to, no matter what that faith is in. All that we have now was given to us by nature. The stones and the vines and the timber that have been forged into weapons and armor will protect us and lead us into battle, but it will be our courage that wins it! It will be our courage that makes us push forward in the face of death! And it will be our courage that sees a new day rise! Ready yourselves, my countrymen. We march to war with the rising sun... we march to war for our kin!"

16

The Bloodstone

"Your friends won't come for you. I can see the hope in your eyes. You believe they will come and save you, but know very well that it is difficult." Ian listened to Vidion's words as he hung by his arms; his feet bound together, and his mouth sealed tight with a cloth. Below him, his feet dangled over the edge of Vidion's castle. They waited on the roof of the oldest tower in the castle, where Vidion repeatedly struck him across the face and body. Sid stood closely to Vidion, chuckling at Ian's misfortune. Across from Ian, another prisoner dangled over the edge in the same way, except that prisoner had a white hood over his head. When the wooziness and tears subsided from his eyes, Ian took a good look at Sid, who he recognized after a few moments. He began to recall the things Sid did to them as kids, especially to his son, Pike. Shortly after that, Ian began to try and struggle free to get his hands on him. Both Vidion and Sid laughed at him as he grew tired and short of breath from trying to escape.

"You won't break free from it, boy. Not from my curse. Not someone as weak and pathetic as you. But I offer a way out.

All you have to do is tell me. Tell me where my brother is and tell me about the scrolls. I know they exist, and I know he has them," said Vidion. Ian hung there, wondering how exactly it was that Vidion had learned of the scrolls. Elona had spent her entire life hiding them from him, and to his knowledge, Laik and his friends were the only ones who knew of their existence. Vidion removed the rag for a moment, so that Ian could reply.

"I... I don't know what you speak of." Vidion smirked at his lie.

"Do you perhaps need a reminder?" suggested Vidion as he sealed his mouth shut again and walked over to the other side of the stronghold. The hooded person lifted their head as if they heard the approaching footsteps of Vidion. As the King grasped the hood, he looked over at Ian, whose eyes were closing from a lack of rest, food, and water. Sid walked over to him and, with pleasure, struck him in the ribs. Ian coughed and gasped for his breath and, in the midst of that, locked eyes with Vidion. Vidion unhooded the figure, only to reveal an even weaker and feebler Flint. The cloth that kept Flint silent was removed for enough time to explain himself to Ian.

"I'm sorry, Ian. I'm sorry. I am old, and I am weak. I swore never to tell anyone about the scrolls, and I haven't until now. I am only thankful for never having read them. I have mentioned nothing more... Be strong, Ian. Vidion knows Laik will come. He plans on killing me in front of my nephew. It's okay, Ian... It's my time. It's my time."

Vidion struck him once more and hooded him again. Ian began to flail around like a fish fighting for its life. He was very fond of Flint, who always took care of him as a child.

"Do you like my plan?" asked Vidion, cynically. Still, Ian refused to tell him anything, and he knew it was precisely what

Flint would have wanted.

As Laik marched toward his older brother, the thought of death grew tenfold. He could not think of anything other than an afterlife. He wondered whether or not any of his loved ones were watching over him, like Elona used to tell him. It was especially difficult to believe at a moment where death was almost certain for him and his men. From the top of a hillside, all who were able to fight took their positions and waited for Laik's command. The Aroku stood there like statues, staring right at them without a speck of fear. Naturally, this intimidated some of the men, who shook in their leather armor. They grasped their weapons so tight that some of them got splinters or blisters, but the pain was ignored.

"What the hell is wrong with him?" whispered Gamet to Pike. Laik stared at the Aroku in plain sight as if he were invisible. He had a blank, dead look on his face; his body still hurt from his encounter with Gronlin. Pike walked forward to meet him, and before he could get a word out, Laik gave his first and only command.

"The rising is yours to command, Pike. Give them the signal when you are ready. They will charge when you wave your hatchets. Your word and your strategy will serve as good as mine. When you attack, I will use the distraction to make my way over the walls of the keep. Ian is in there somewhere, and the sooner I act, the better chance we have for his safe return... I will not let him die too. No matter the cost." Pike understood and nodded his head. Shortly after, Laik made his way downhill, concealed by the shrubs and trees which led to the side of the castle's moat. The moat was filled with Vidion's Aroku, who were still staring at the rebels.

"What was that about?" asked Gamet.

"I can't believe I just agreed to that. He just left to face Vidion on his own," responded Pike, with confusion all over his face.

Gamet choked on his drink and answered, "What?! Are you serious, Pike? We need to follow him!"

Iolas took note of the commotion and walked over to calm the situation down. He could see the fuss began to make the men a bit antsy, especially since they did not know what they were speaking about.

"What's the matter, folks? The men are getting nervous here. You should probably try to calm down a bit," Iolas suggested.

Pike turned to Iolas to advise him of the current predicament.

"Your brother thought it would be wise to fight Vidion on his own. He left and asked me to make the calls! How the hell am I supposed to know when the right time to attack is? Those rocks are looking at us like Gamet looks at his food!" As he shared the news with Iolas, the men watched carefully for the signal. By pure coincidence, Pike began to wave his arms like a mad man, and although he wasn't aware of it, he was currently grasping a hatchet in each of his hands. Confused and unsure, the army began to charge toward the Aroku, and, as one, the horde drew their weapons.

"Oh, crud! What did I do?" yelled Pike. "Iolas... you stay and lead them! They know you, and they will follow you! Gamet... let's fight our way into the castle! Laik needs our help!" commanded Pike.

As they fought through the landslide of fiends, Moki continuously jumped from Gamet's shoulder to the heads of the enemy and back. It was nothing but a tap to the monsters, but the distraction was enough to allow Gamet and Pike to use their newly found weapons to their advantage. It still was not easy to stop the Aroku, but the weapons Iolas had given them were much stronger than those the rest of their men had to use. Then, amid the struggle, Pike caught a glimpse of what appeared to be the man leading the horde. As Pike got closer to the figure, the steam and fog that rose from the magma under the hot grounds became easier to see through. Gamet caught sight of the figure as well, and shouted,

"Go! I'll hold off these rocks while you stop their commander." Stopping him would give them an advantage. There would be no more order on their side, and the Aroku would continue to fight blindly. Gamet thrashed and bashed through each of the monsters that came his way, although it took great force and effort with his hammer. While Gamet worked on reducing the flow where they stood, Pike finally reached the commander of the Aroku, after crushing two of them on his own. His back was turned toward Pike and he was standing only a few paces away from him. Lucky for him, Pike enjoyed a fight and took pride in fighting fair. Pike called out to the man, and as he turned to face him, Pike's heart sank, and his chest suddenly clenched tightly.

It was his father, Sid. The same man who had physically abused him as a child and the same man who had killed his mother. The look on Sid's face changed as he recognized that the person who called to him was his son. It became a look of shame, of panic, and of terror. They had not seen each other in nearly twenty years, but the anguish that his father had caused felt as fresh as if his mother was murdered the day before. "You!" yelled Pike the moment he recognized who he was. "Ahhh!" Pike roared as he paced back and forth, wanting nothing but his father's head. Sid grew intensely nervous, completely unaware of his surroundings, and scared to the bone. In a slick attempt to use his manipulative ways to get out of his predicament, Sid opened his mouth to convince his son to let him go. But before he could get two words out, Pike charged at him with his hatchets.

"You! You bastard!"

Pike swung and slashed his father from head to toe. The gashes on his face and body were deep and wide, each bleeding profusely. His father now lay on the ground, looking up at Pike, knowing that his death was near, but it was not enough for Pike. He wanted him dead; now. Sid tried his best to utter a few meaningless words to his son, but once again, before he could speak, Pike repeatedly began to crush his face as he yelled the word 'die!' with every stomp. His father was dead, but despite the fact, Pike continued to stomp on him until Gamet grabbed hold of him and dragged him out of danger. Both of them hid inside the entrance of the castle to regain composure. At the same time, the rest of the men continued to fight against the Aroku.

Iolas was now overwhelmed by the horde, and all of his commands and strategies were proving to be useless. They were still too many, and they were too strong for their weapons of nature. The monsters continuously spawned from the land, fueled by the core of their world. For every beast that fell, two surfaced from the ground. In the east, the last of the men crossed over the hill and entered the war zone. In the south, Iolas could see the majority of the army fighting their way toward him. Still, in the north, where he stood, the Aroku had all but taken over. Very few of the rebels still stood fighting. Iolas continued to fight and defend, and just before the club of one of the fiends would have crushed his head, one of his men bashed its arm with a heavy rock. Its arm was shattered into pieces, and the bits flew into Iolas' eyes, rendering him nearly useless for a few moments.

All hope seemed to be lost, but as his blurred vision began to clear, Iolas noticed what appeared to be an army on top of the western valley. As he tried his best to clear his eyes and squint for a better view, he found that it was indeed an army, but there was something peculiar about their shape and stature. It was an army of apples, and they were irate. The ambush of Leaflake had resulted in the loss of their home, the only tree that was large enough for them, and the only one that was enchanted with the power to preserve them all.

Although the Aroku were sturdy and large, they were quite dumb. The presence of the apples baffled them, and their attention turned to them. Two of the men helped Iolas into the castle and out of danger, because he could not see very well. The bunch of fruit charged without fear, and when they met with the Aroku, they began to bounce and jump from fiend to fiend. The monsters started to slowly destroy themselves, smashing and bashing at each other as they tried to get the apples. Some of the apples did indeed perish as the Aroku swung their heavy arms to swat them away like flies. The men took advantage of the situation and charged with all of the will and might they had left. With the fiends distracted, they were able to engage and fight against the horde with greater ease. As the battle began to balance, the apples took note of the fact that a dam was the one thing allowing the Aroku to continue growing.

A few of the apples headed toward the dam, taking a few of the men with them. Iolas managed to wash his eyes out in a fountain. From deep inside the fortress, Iolas could hear the yelling coming from what sounded like Pike. Iolas dried his face and headed toward the direction of the holler, but before he could find him, a large, thick, heavy door closed right before him. The sound of Pike's voice could not be heard any more, and the only sound Iolas was able to hear was the sound of the door being barricaded on the other side.

It was Gamet who secured the door, and Pike and Gamet were unaware that Iolas was on the other side. The ruckus that Iolas made by knocking and banging on the door became alarming to them, and they figured it was likely the Aroku that were after them. Gamet grabbed Pike, who was still in shock and angry after killing his father.

Moki jumped onto Pike's shoulder and began licking the tears off his blank face.

"Pike! Pike! You must snap out of it. He's dead. You avenged your mother! Laik is in here somewhere and needs our help," Gamet explained. The look on Pike's face remained unchanged. Gamet cocked an open hand back, and before smacking him across the face, he once again yelled, "Pike!"

The slap left a ringing in his ear, but it was enough to bring Pike back to focus. Moki jumped back onto Gamet's shoulder, and they quickly made their way further into the castle. After checking room after room for their friend, they entered a large room that seemed to have been recently destroyed. It was the great hall. Some of the pillars were toppled over. The walls were cracked as if perhaps someone had thrown the pillars against them. At the other end of the room, a broad staircase led to the upper floors, but before they could reach it, the silence of the room became no more. A loud growl and heavy steps could be heard and felt just behind them, and an even stronger stench overcame their senses before looking behind their shoulders.

It was Klokus, the protector of the gods' tomb.

"Go! Get out of here! Find Laik! I will stop this foul beast!" yelled Gamet. Laik needed help, and they knew it. Although

Klokus was fierce and vicious, there was no one more powerful than Vidion himself. Pike hated the idea of leaving Gamet alone. He knew that he was unlikely to stop a beast as powerful as Klokus all on his own, but the most important matter at the moment was Laik. The fall of Vidion had to be ensured.

Pike ran up the steps to find him after shouting out, "I love you, Gamet! Watch yourself!"

Gamet remained looking forward, locking eyes with Klokus as he whispered under his breath, "I love you too, my brother. Until we meet again."

At the top of the fortress, both Ian and Flint still hung helplessly over the edge. Vidion paced back and forth slowly in anticipation of his brother's arrival, and before long, the door that led to the rooftop slowly creaked open.

"My brother," said Vidion with confidence.

Laik walked forward with caution and looked at his surroundings. There appeared to be nothing out of the ordinary, except the man who hung over the edge was hooded. Laik looked at the opposite end, still watching out for a sudden attack from his brother, and noticed his friend Ian.

"Let him go, Vidion. I'm here. Let him leave," said Laik. Ian recognized the voice and lifted his head with the little strength he had left to see him. Tears began to race across his cheek, but it was not for his life or out of fear. It was for Laik's uncle, Flint.

"Lucky for you, little brother, you will have the choice to save him... You see, I don't believe in what our grandmother told us. The gods don't exist. I've been telling you since you were a little boy, but you never took my word for it. If the gods were real, a bolt of lightning would strike me dead where I stand, and you would leave with both of them... but no. This is the real world, and I have the advantage. You can choose, Laik. You can choose which one you would like to save; your friend Ian or this man under the hood; an innocent bystander," said Vidion. Ian began to mumble and struggled to break free once again. Laik paid no mind to whatever it was that he was trying to say because, in his mind, Ian was likely trying to tell him to save the prisoner. He was selfless like that, and Laik knew it. The only thing Laik did not know was that the man under the hood was his uncle.

Laik thought for a few moments, trying to find a way out of the situation. Right behind Vidion, he could see that a lever to release each of them was within Vidion's grasp, so attacking him would not have been wise.

"Choose quickly, or both will die," Vidion demanded. Ian continued to squirm and yell through the cloth as he desperately tried to warn Laik that the other man was his uncle. After observing the hooded man, Laik noticed that the man was not moving. He figured that he was likely weak and unconscious or possibly dead. The thought of saving him began to seem pointless, especially since he was not sure if he was alive. On the other hand, one of his closest friends dangled over certain death.

"Ian! Let Ian live. Please...just let him go. You have taken nearly everyone from me. You can give me that, at least," begged Laik. Vidion grinned and safely released Ian, knowing that the choice would not go well for Laik either way. After all, it was Vidion's purpose to be rid of everyone he loved. Laik carefully walked over to Ian, and cautiously unbound his feet and arms. At the same time, Vidion prepared to cut the hooded man loose. Ian was severely hurt, and even the removal of the ropes felt like a dagger through his back. As Laik removed the cloth from Ian's mouth, Ian gasped for air and wailed,

"Laik! Stop! Take me! That man is your uncle! It's Flint!"

Vidion snipped the line at the sound of his yelp and down fell Flint to his death. The hood came off in mid-air, and his body crashed against the floor. His lifeless body lay at the bottom. Laik rushed over to the edge to see if it were true, and the sight of his deceased uncle killed him inside. *I killed him*, he thought to himself, and his choice once again brought him to a state where he could not focus clearly.

"What's the matter, brother? Is it my armor? Does it intimidate you? My helmet is made from the skull of your father. Does it irk you, brother?" Vidion laughed out loud, mocking his younger brother, and drew the sword of the king, the last steel blade in existence. Laik's rage flared up, and he unsheathed his sword, the armor wrapping around him for his protection. Vidion was briefly shaken by the sight of it because, before their weapons clashed, he realized that Laik was holding the sword of the gods, The Bloodstone.

17

The Unknown

By this time, the men were losing the battle. The Aroku continued to grow, and it felt as if two of them were spawning from the ground for every one that was killed. The apples, and the men that followed them, had finally reached the dam that kept the water from flowing around the moat. Although it was strong, the dam was old and had its weak points. Parts of it were made of wood, which had rotted over the years. The men hacked away at the old wood with their stone axes, while the apples chewed and gnawed on the old timber. Rotting wood was, coincidentally, a favorite food of theirs. After much effort, the dam cracked open, and the water made its way into the moat. Most of the cold water made its way underground, where the magma cooled and solidified. The rest of it created a shallow, shin-deep, and swamp-like grave where the dead rested.

The spawning of the Aroku was finally put to a stop. Between the army of apples and the army of men, a victory began to look possible. Still, unfortunately, the struggle between monster and man did not end there. Inside the castle, Gamet fought hard against the mighty Klokus on his own.

Klokus managed to smash over nearly all of the pillars in the great hall, but one pillar in the center kept the roof from collapsing on them. The only way Gamet was able to strike the beast was by striking him on his back while Moki distracted him. There was no doubt in Gamet's mind. Had it not been for Moki, he would likely have succumbed to Klokus within the first few minutes.

"Moki... Moki!" called Gamet. Moki hobbled over to him as fast as he could. "Do you see that pillar in the center? We need to get him to topple it over. It's the only way I can see us getting out of this. He is much too strong for us, but if we could get the ceiling to collapse on him, we might be able to stop him."

Moki understood, and headed toward the pillar. Klokus viciously turned the larger pieces of debris over and searched around for the slightest scent of them. Moki finally reached the pillar in the center and made as much noise as he possibly could, eventually catching the attention of the beast. The creature roared loud and deep as it charged at Moki and crashed against the pillar. Although it fell over and the ceiling began to slowly cave in, Klokus paid no mind to it and got up to pursue Moki. Gamet raced over to his friend, who was now cornered by the beast, and once he reached him, he swung his ax into its lower back as hard as he could. Klokus shrieked so loud that Gamet's eardrums nearly burst. Moki was saved for only a moment as Klokus turned to Gamet and slammed him against the stone wall. He lay next to Moki with a few broken ribs, and in his last act of defense, he flung his ax toward Klokus, striking him in the throat. The monster took a few steps back, unable to breathe as its blood poured from its wound. The ceiling began to collapse on all of them, and Gamet turned to shield his tiny friend. The large pieces of rock and stone had finally fallen and crushed those who stood below it.

Pike could feel the trembling from the top of what felt like a never-ending staircase as he got closer and closer to the end. At the top, just down the hall, he could see the rooftop entrance where Laik must have been. Ian, on the other hand, remained on the ground hurt and nearly unconscious.

Laik ran toward Vidion with his sword first. His sword skills stunned Vidion, who backed away as often as he could to avoid a fatal strike. Vidion's armor, made from the bones of Toewood's graves, was cursed and strong enough to resist the average sword, but against The Bloodstone, it remained untested. Despite his impressive skills with the blade, Vidion could see that Laik was hurt from his previous battle, and it was an advantage he was prepared to use. Vidion knocked him off of his feet with a gust of wind and chased him with several strikes of his steel blade. Laik rolled away as fast as he could, and before he knew it, found himself pressed against a stone wall. The evil king thrust his sword forward, but just before it impaled him, Laik sprung out of the way, and into the stone Vidion's sword went.

Pike had reached them just a few seconds before, saw this as an opportunity, and sprinted toward Ian. He picked him up and took him inside, where he would be away from danger. Laik then swung his sword at Vidion's arm in an attempt to chop it off, but he was too swift to receive the hit. Instead, Laik found his blade stuck in the stone as well, but he would not have the same luck. He let go of the sword, and with it, his armor went. Vidion pulled his steel blade from the wall and stabbed his brother through the stomach. Down Laik fell and rested against the wall, which was smeared in his blood.

"Laik!" yelled Pike as he charged toward Vidion, but Vidion

nearly gusted him off of the edge of the tower, and barricaded him with a wall of fire.

"Elona always told you not to worry. She told you that we would all meet again once we die, and here you are. The moment you have feared your entire life is here; your death... Are you scared, my little brother? Do you believe in the afterlife?" teased Vidion. The sword of the gods stared Vidion in the eyes. With it, the end of the human race was just within his hands, and it was what Vidion desired most. Pike watched helplessly as the fire began to slowly push him back and off of the ledge.

"Elona only told you these things to make you feel safe. She never believed in the gods or spirituality. She only believed in the weak-minded, like you. The thoughts of an afterlife are for those who are too afraid of death. They believe they are significant to this world, and their ego does not let them go in peace, but we are worthless, Laik. We are worthless," Vidion continued. Laik's spirit was crushed by the words from his brother. Even though he felt certain Elona had not spoken those words, Vidion was right. There was nothing more that Laik feared than the moment that seemed to have arrived. "You robbed me, Laik. When you kept the ashes of Erthos from me, you slowed me down. Your soul could have been at peace right now, along with your loved ones... but this sword is all that I need now, and you brought it to me. You are the reason everyone left in this world will fall. I will become a real god."

Laik tried to reach for the sword, but he was too weak to do anything. This, of course, would have been the perfect opportunity for Laik to use his magic, but his powers were useless from where he stood. The nearest sediments of Erthos were too far to control. Closest to him were the walls that surrounded the castle, and beyond that was a moat that had become a shallow grave, nothing but rock beneath it. Vidion placed his foot on top of Laik's hand, crushing his fingers to the bone. Vidion smirked at the sight of his brother in pain and cynically leaned into mutter, "Where are your gods now?"

Vidion grasped the hilt of The Bloodstone, but just as he pulled, the sword turned to ashes in his palm. The ashes hit the ground, and Vidion watched as the sword reformed once again. It was to Vidion's disbelief, but the dark sorcerer tried to wield it once more, only to discover that the sword disintegrated just as before. "What is this?!" he roared as he turned to face his brother. Laik coughed to clear his throat of blood and shared the words Vidion did not wish to hear.

"You do not share the blood of my father... You are no god."

The words drove Vidion insane, and all the while, Pike had readied his bow and arrows within the flames that imprisoned him. Pike shot the arrows at Vidion one by one as he grabbed his steel blade and began to stomp his way toward him. He shot as his life began to flash before his eyes, for if it were not to be a death at the hands of the sorcerer, then it was a fall to his certain death. The arrows bounced off of Vidion's armor and did no harm to him, and as Vidion closed the distance between them, he raised his sword for a fatal blow. The sword pierced through his heart, and to his knees he fell, but it was not Pike who was impaled; it was Vidion.

Vidion dropped to the ground before him, and Iolas was flung away because of a surge of power. Iolas tumbled to a stop and rose from the ground with The Bloodstone still in his hand. The rain began to fall heavily, and the flames that imprisoned Pike were soon extinguished. Both Iolas and Pike ran toward Laik, who had witnessed the whole thing. Iolas carefully placed his head on his lap as Pike grabbed his hand in an attempt to help him feel at ease.

"Laik. Hang on. We are here; your brother and I. Stay with us, Laik. It's over; it's all over," said Pike as Laik cleared his throat of blood once more. "...I am at peace now... my brothers... There is no darkness in death. There is... no darkness... in death."

His lifeless stare sent tears down their faces as they watched the rain wash away his blood. Pike followed the river of blood, which fell off of the edge like a waterfall. At the end of it, he could see that the rebellion had won the war. Very few of the Aroku were still alive, and the men outnumbered them with ease. Still, the structure of the tower did not seem safe, and Iolas and Pike picked up their brothers Laik and Ian, carrying them out of danger. It was difficult because the castle was immense, their bodies were limp, and both Iolas and Pike were beaten and exhausted. Every room was filled with debris and the bodies of both the Aroku and their men. Some were even flooded because of the heavy rain that mixed with the blood of the dead.

"Wait," Pike called as he tried to catch his breath. His legs gave out on him and he was forced to place Ian down. The walls and ceiling once again began to cave in, and the two of them looked at one another as if they knew it was their final moment.

"I'm not leaving them," said Pike.

"And neither am I," exclaimed Iolas, as he sat back and appeared to accept his fate. From within the next room, the deep bellow of a beast echoed, and Pike closed his eyes, preparing himself to be mauled by whatever came.

Iolas wobbled to his feet, and unsheathed The Bloodstone, the armor shielding his body. As the monster caught sight of them, it began to charge, but before any of them could react, the head of the beast was met with an ax. Down the monster went, and out came Gamet as he pulled his ax from its head. The men were thrilled to see him, but too weak to show it. Despite his broken ribs, Gamet threw Ian and Laik over his shoulders and helped Pike and Iolas out of the castle safely.

All that was left were the ruins of the once-great stronghold. Still, the rebels celebrated their victory with their weapons raised high in the air.

The following moonlight, the rebels, and all of the villagers who were saved, paid their respects to Laik. They buried him in Toewood, right next to his grandmother Elona. Within a short amount of time, the village thrived like the others that were later built around it, mostly thanks to Gamet's brute strength and assistance from Moki.

Pike visited Laik's grave as often as he could and spoke to him as if he were still alive. It was where he went to vent, and served as an outlet for all of the things that troubled him and kept him up at night. The most reoccurring conversation was, of course, about his father, but one night, Pike took a seat in front of his grave and began to share a few words he never spoke to anyone.

"Hello, my brother. Here I am again. You must be tired of hearing my voice by now. You are probably thinking that I am not letting you rest in peace, wishing that I leave you in peace for once," Pike joked as he chuckled to himself. "The truth is... it's hard for me to let go. I often think about that dreadful night; the night you both left us yet saved us all. I can't help but think that I could have done more to save you. I replay what happened in my mind over and over again and... if I... if I had simply stopped you from going, we could have been here sharing a drink. I don't know why I didn't stop you. I often wish it were me buried here. Then perhaps you would be sitting here crying to me... Anyway, I can't seem to shake off the guilt, and

I wanted to tell you, if you can hear me, that I am sorry. I am sorry that I failed you... but I promise to watch over the people you loved and cared for and to be there for those who need me, no matter the cost. And if a day comes where life is proven to have a purpose, and we meet again, I promise to let you punch me or piss on my face once more for letting you die. I love you, my brother."

Iolas tried his best to remain quiet while Pike finished his prayer but could not help but interrupt after Pike's last remark.

"Piss? On your face? Once more?" he asked with laughter. "You have to tell me about this. Why in the world, or how in the world did he manage to urinate on your face?"

Pike was slightly startled by him but cackled at his reaction.

"That... is a story I can tell you about over some ale. I can share a thousand stories about your brother, and each of them will be just as great as the next. You will see."

Iolas laughed once more and continued to do so until the sun began to set. Not long after, Pike began to wonder if his thoughts were anything like those of Iolas; specifically about life and death. It was something that never seemed to bother Pike, but ever since the death of Laik, the thoughts lingered in his mind.

"Tell me, Iolas. Your brother spent his entire life questioning the existence of the gods. You were there to hear his final words. What do you think of them? 'There is no darkness in death.' What do you think he meant?"

Iolas took a deep breath, unsure of what to say exactly, but the only thing he could share was his personal beliefs. "It's... difficult to say. Some would say that the darkness he spoke of was literal. They say that when you die, everything begins to fade away until you are no more. I like to believe that he found

212

internal peace with his death. You tell me that he struggled with the concept of death until his dying breath because he feared what would happen to him once he left this world... But he never stopped to think that his time here was more important than what happens after. The sons of our fathers only became great men because their fathers were great men, and they, in turn, raised Laik the same way. Without the goodness of their hearts, there wouldn't be a today. I guess what I'm saying is... everything you do in life has a purpose; there is a reason for living, and there is a reason for dying. An immortal life would only bring men greed, and they would lose the value of life, the same value that Laik tried to hang on to so desperately... He loved life. I believe Laik realized that as he passed on. He realized that he could not be greedy and that the time that is given to us in this world must be shared with others. We will never know what happens after death... but I believe he is in a better place. I believe he is no longer in darkness."

About the Author

J.S. Torres is a Science Teacher and author of The Bloodstone: The Leaf and the Tree of Old, which is his debut novel. He first began writing and creating other worlds and stories in the third grade, but never published until now. Although J.S. Torres lives in Florida, he was born in San Francisco, California and loves the outdoors. One of his goals in life is to visit all of the U.S. National Parks. During his free time, he enjoys diving into his hobbies and spending time with his three boys Zachary, Adam and Matthew.